PRAISE FOR BONKERS

"A fun, funny, and gripping read and, like all Patrick Carman books, full of memorable characters that suck you into a wonderfully weird, layered world . . . It all adds up to a fabulously good time."
—JOE PURDY,
TV animation writer for
Arthur, *Llama Llama*, and *Hey Arnold!*

"This book is gross, hilarious, chaotic, funny, and scary . . . Maybe it's the madcap plot, maybe it's the deadpan humor, or maybe it's the tale of friendship at its core, but this book grabbed me and didn't let go. I can't wait for the next installment!"
—STEPHEN BRAMUCCI,
award-winning author of the Danger Gang series

"Patrick Carman is a lovely and kind man with a wacko sense of imagination. I couldn't have imagined this tale if I had fifty lifetimes to think about it. It's wild, funny, outlandish, and outrageous. Boy, does it move!!! Take the wild ride. It's a blast!"
—RICHARD KIND,
actor

"This book is the pits! And I mean that in the best way. So much laugh-out-loud fun and adventures from one armpit! I love this series—you'll go Bonkers, too!"

—R. L. STINE,
author of Goosebumps and Fear Street

"This suspenseful and hilarious Bonkers adventure has it all: embarrassing underarm problems, a mysterious abandoned lab where all the wacky and gross trouble starts, and three wisecracking friends trying to figure it all out. Patrick Carman knows exactly what tickles the funny bones for kids!"

—RACHEL LIPMAN,
Emmy Award–winning writer/producer of
Rugrats, *Recess*, and *Sabrina the Teenage Witch*

THE TERROR IN JENNY'S ARMPIT

BOOKS BY PATRICK CARMAN

BONKERS!

THE TERROR IN JENNY'S ARMPIT

PATRICK CARMAN

BLACK STONE
PUBLISHING

Printed in the United States of America

First edition: 2024
ISBN 979-8-212-53837-4
Juvenile Fiction / Horror

Version 1

Blackstone Publishing
31 Mistletoe Rd.
Ashland, OR 97520

www.BlackstonePublishing.com

This one is for my dad.

TABLE OF CONTENTS

THE TERROR IN
JENNY'S ARMPIT

CHAPTER 1

HOW DID THIS HAPPEN?!
ALSO, CAN WE BE FRIENDS?

Something is wrong with my armpit.

Normally I wouldn't even mention it be-cause I'm prone to injuries in the first place, so what's the big deal, right? I mean just last week I walked into the patio door and when I got up off the ground, I was sure my elbow had fallen off. Nope, it was still attached, swelling up like a watermelon.

And don't even get me started about what happened when I jumped off the roof of the house with an umbrella for a parachute. Hey, you take a dare, you live with the consequences, right? A rose bush broke my fall, and I survived with a few dozen scratches. I lived to stumble into trouble another day! I've tripped on toys, rode my bike into a tree, and cracked my head on a table (don't ask). And that's just in the past three days.

But this is different.

There is definitely something wrong with my armpit.

Itch level: fourteen out of ten.

It's possible an angry kitten is living in there.

Before I get too far into this, I'll be honest: an armpit is a private matter that should only be discussed with your closest friends. A lot goes on in your average armpit, very little of it good, so you should only talk with your bestie about what's happening in there. Given that I'm short on time because I really need to figure out what's wrong with my armpit as fast as I can, I'll tell you a little bit about me and then we'll jump right into being friends for life.

My name is Jenny and I live in a strange little town that's not on the way to anywhere. We've been told to avoid talking about our town because a lot of curious things happen here, and the adults would rather not have a bunch of gawkers and news vans showing up making a big stink over every little thing. Let's call my town . . . Nevermind.

Nevermind, nothing to see here, pay no attention to us.

Yeah, that'll work.

Here are five things about me that will help us get to know each other better:

1. I am eleven years old.
2. I'm not clumsy, I'm adventurous. There's a difference!
3. I always wear high-tops (to protect my ankles), cargo shorts (for carrying

snacks and stuff), and my lucky mood ring. I know what you're thinking. Is it *really* a lucky mood ring? Because if it was, wouldn't I have avoided the patio door, stuck the rooftop-umbrella landing, and dodged the tree on my bike? Hey, I survived all those failburgs! My mood ring is lucky city.

4. I like to make up words. Like failburg.

5. I like making lists.

And there we go! We are now friends for life, so let's talk more about me.

I live in a white house with a blue door, and while I'm not an only child I might as well be. I have two brothers, but they're both in high school and they basically ignore me 90 percent of the time. A few weeks ago, I invited them both to watch me jump over my mom's car with my bike and neither one of them showed up, so you see what I'm dealing with here. My brothers will be no help with my current problem.

"Jenny! Hurry up your breakfast is getting cold!"

That would be my mom yelling from downstairs. I don't even need to be in the kitchen to know she's pouring coffee into a travel mug, grabbing a banana, and heading for the door. Wait for it . . .

"Don't get into any trouble today! Also I love you and you're the greatest!"

And there it is. Same script, new day. *Don't get into any trouble* has become her go-to Jedi mind trick when she leaves for her office. I don't want you to take this the wrong way, but I have been known to let my adventurous nature get me into some tricky situations. Like pole-vaulting over a card table with a yard rake (I ended up under the card table).

But Jenny, what about your dad, couldn't he help you with your armpit problem?

Okay, for starters, I can't believe you would even ask that. There is no way I'm letting my dad examine my armpit. Besides, while my dad works from home every day, he's not even going to be awake until I'm long gone for school because he's a computer programmer. Translation: he really gets cookin' after midnight, not a minute sooner, and rarely rises before noon. Just last night he dragged me into his office to explain something about robots hiding web pages and something called robot.txt and honestly, the whole thing was a blur.

Moving on!

You should know that I hardly ever think about my armpit at all. In fact, until I woke up this morning, I hadn't thought about my armpit in weeks. Maybe my armpit is mad because it's being ignored, but I'm pretty sure body parts don't work like that. I haven't paid any attention to my belly button in at least a month, and it hasn't complained once.

What we need to do is conduct a good old-fashioned investigation, starting with what this thing looks like. Hang on.

I have now looked in a mirror, and there does not appear to be a small angry cat living in my armpit, so that's a relief. Now for the bad news— there's a blotchy red spot in there, and I think it's possible it was looking at me. I say this because while I was staring at it, the red blotch got a little redder and then it started itching again so I scratched it. Scratching it might have been a mistake, because when I did that, something really gross happened.

The blotch in my armpit made a sound.

CHAPTER 2

FEN STENSON AND
BARKER MIFFLIN

The sound I heard was like when a rabbit eats celery—or, as I like to say, when Bun-Bun eats snuffle sticks. I used to have an imaginary rabbit called Bun-Bun, and it ate a lot of celery, which I call snuffle. If I can imagine a pet bunny and its favorite snacks, there's a chance I could be imagining this whole noisy blotch thing, and my armpit is just fine. I'm glad we're friends because if we weren't friends, I'm pretty sure you'd be saying to yourself, *This Jenny character is a real pinhead. I think I'll find a new friend.* But you would never do that, right?

Let the investigation continue!

Did anything happen yesterday that could explain the terror in my armpit?

Let's start at the breakfast table, where my two caveman brothers show up every morning and eat anything that's not nailed down. I try to avoid this daily scene of food-eating mayhem as often as I can, but yesterday morning I was there while they ate seven bowls of cereal between them and fought over the last bagel like two hyenas. They've been pro wrestling fans since they were toddlers, so things quickly escalated into a Battle of the Bagel cage match. They nearly kicked a hole in the television, one of them did a flying jackhammer onto the sofa in the living room, and a perfectly good lampshade was crushed into my brother's face. My brother's face won.

On the bright side, I enjoyed the show while I ate the bagel they were fighting over.

Could a bagel cause an armpit rash? This seems unlikely, but I'm not ruling it out. Mr. Bagel, you are suspect number one!

While I was walking to school, Fen Stenson rolled up on his scooter and started yammering at my face. Fen is a new kid in town, and he always shows up on his scooter at the corner at the same time every morning. It's like he's watching me from a distance, and when I make the turn toward school, he kicks it into high gear and races over so he doesn't have to enter the building all alone. Fen's scooter has an annoying squeak from a recent accident, like one of those shopping carts at the store with a bum wheel. It's possible Fen Stenson likes me.

Typical Fen small talk took place while the scooter squeaked annoyingly down the pavement.

"Jenster! How we doin' today?"

"I'm Jenny. And you are?"

"Ah Jen-Jen, you crack me up."

"No one here is called Jen-Jen."

"So what we up to after school? I'm thinking we share headphones and sample the latest Swedish beats."

"I barely understand what you just said, but I'm jumping over my mom's car on my bike after school. You can watch if you want to."

"Kid Lawn Dart rides again! I'm sure it'll turn out better than last time."

He's talking about when I borrowed his scooter and tried to jump over a garbage can. The scooter ended up hanging from a limb in a tree—I still don't understand how that happened—and it's had that squeaky wheel ever since. Oh, and Kid Lawn Dart is my daredevil name. Because lawn darts are dangerous!

I don't think talking to Fen Stenson is the cause of my problem, but I'm not going to check it off my list until I'm 100 percent sure. In case details about said suspect are useful, here is basically everything I know about Fen Stenson:

1. He's originally from Sweden, or at least his parents are.
2. Fen is trying to introduce Swedish dance music at school. It's not going very well.
3. Fen dresses like a manga comic book cosplay, including styling his hair like famous manga character Kakashi Hatake (long, spiked, and blond).
4. He occasionally covers his face with a mask, and often wears a headband.
5. Fen will tag along on just about any adventure, a fun hang, low maintenance.

I can't think of anything that happened at school that could have caused the terror in my armpit, so let's jump right to the end of the day when I was walking back toward my house with another friend of mine, Barker Mifflin.

"Are we doing this or what?" Barker said.

"I don't know, are we?" I asked.

"Gotta have total agreement about going in," Barker said. "We're out of the planning stage now, into the real deal."

Barker Mifflin was talking about a plan to explore the old Colossal Chemistry building at the edge of town, something we'd been talking about doing for weeks. And he was right. The planning was long gone. We were just stalling at this point.

"Are you sure it's cool?" I asked for the four hundredth time.

"I'm telling you, Jenny, we're cool," Barker said in his most assuring voice. "The place has been abandoned for over a year now. Aren't you curious what they were doing in there?"

"They *were* totally sneakretive in that place," I agreed.

"Sneakretive . . . Oh, I got it! Sneaky *and* secretive," said Barker.

"You're sure you have a way in that doesn't break any rules?" I asked.

"One hundred percent. I've reconned the entire outer edge of the property. They've completely abandoned the place."

"I do love a good adventure," I said.

I looked at Barker and I was immediately reminded that he's sort of an oddball. Barker Mifflin is an eleven-year-old survivalist wannabe who never leaves home without a go bag strapped to his back. It's full of ropes and strange hand tools, water bottles and ziplocked containers of food rations. He wears army boots, camo pants, and fingerless gloves. And he's probably the most suspicious kid I know. At the very top of Barker Mifflin's list of suspicious things in the town of Nevermind is Colossal Chemistry.

While I was thinking about whether or not to sneak into the old Colossal Chemistry site, I heard a squeaky wheel approaching.

Fen Stenson rolled up beside me.

"Kid Lawn Dart!" said Fen. "Hey, Barker."

"Hey," said Barker.

Fen had only met Barker Mifflin once before and the two of them were still sizing each other up. I'd known Barker for years and knew he was nervous around new kids. It usually took some time for him to trust people. So here I was, stuck between two very different classmates. Fen Stenson, who was all about making new friends in a new place; and Barker Mifflin, who was more of a loner.

"Change of plans," I said, because now there were three of us and three felt like the right number for exploring an abandoned chemistry lab. "I forgot my mom drove her car to work so the Kid Lawn Dart show will have to wait until this weekend."

"That's cool," said Fen. His wheel kept squeaking until Barker couldn't stand it anymore.

"I'm going to need you to step off the scooter," Barker said.

"No problem!" said Fen. "Jen-Jen got it stuck in a tree recently, but it's a good ride."

"I'm Jenny," I said. "We've talked about this."

Barker dug around in his backpack full of weird tools and pulled out a hammer.

"What's the hammer for?" asked Fen.

The hammer clobbered the front wheel of the scooter several times. Fen's jaw dropped, but to his credit, he didn't say anything as Barker got out some pliers and turned a screw. He squeezed something goopy looking from a tube into the center of the front wheel, then threw all his tools back into his pack and flung it over his shoulder.

"Let's get a move on," said Barker, "Time's a wasting." He started walking again.

Fen Stenson boarded the scooter and it wheeled along as silent as a soft breeze.

"Hey, you fixed the squeak!" Fen said. "I'm not gonna lie, it's a better outcome than I expected. Where are we going again?"

Barker looked at me. "Can we trust this kid?"

"Oh, you can trust me," Fen said. "I'm very trustable."

This was my last chance to say no, but I nodded quietly and we picked up our pace as we passed the turn off to my house.

"It's go time," I said.

"Go time?" asked Fen. "What's go time?"

And that's when I said the words that I think might have something to do with the terror in my armpit.

"We're sneaking into Colossal Chemistry."

CHAPTER 3

COLOSSAL CHEMISTRY

As I sit at the kitchen table eating a breakfast burrito, it's time to take an inventory of the possible reasons for the terror in my armpit.

So far, I have identified the following potential answers:

1. The bagel I ate for breakfast yesterday morning did it.
2. Bun-Bun is living in my armpit eating snuffle sticks.

These don't seem likely, or even reasonable, but our investigation of yesterday has taken a new turn. We have reached the gates of Colossal Chemistry, where I think we'll make better progress. Maybe if I retrace my steps, something will jog my memory. The quest for answers continues!

Here's what I remember about Colossal Chemistry.

Barker Mifflin led us all the way around the campus. Being a very sneakretive place, there's a fourteen-foot-tall wall around the entire site with only one entrance.

"We passed the front doors somewhere back there," I said as Barker led us farther along the wall. "Isn't that the only entrance?"

"It's boarded up," said Barker. "And I'm pretty sure there's a laser security system. If we try to go that way, we might trigger some sort of alarm."

"I thought they were all gone?" Fen said. He

had his scooter thrown over his back, held by a shoulder strap covered in anime patches.

"I'm not so sure," Barker said. "I've seen the old security vans driving around here, making sure it's sealed up good and tight. And there's a website."

"A website?" I asked. Barker Mifflin was probably overreacting, but he was also really smart. Maybe Colossal Chemistry still had people hanging around.

"It's probably nothing," said Barker. "Just someone who used to work here who has some worries."

"Worries?" Fen said. "What kind of worries?"

"Here we are," said Barker.

Barker was standing in front of a hole in the ground with a grate covering it.

"Please tell me this isn't your plan," I said.

Barker started digging around in his go bag.

"This is the plan."

"I thought we agreed you weren't going to say that."

"I never agreed to that."

"It's a sewer pipe," I said. "And this is a terrible idea."

"Not a sewer pipe," Barker corrected as he pried the grate off the opening. He tossed it aside and looked into the hole. "It's a drainpipe. I'm pretty sure it connects to one of the lower levels inside."

Fen stuck his head in the hole. "Anyone down there?"

His voice echoed like the hole was deeper than I'd hoped.

"I'll go first. You two follow me," Barker said. He attached a light to his head and turned it on. "Into the belly of the beast."

Before I could think of a good reason not to climb into the hole, Barker was already halfway down the metal ladder. The kid could really move. Thinking back on it now, there were at least three things I could have said at that point:

1. There's probably a badger den or a skunk family at the bottom of this hole.
2. There could be zombies at the bottom of this hole.
3. There is something at the bottom of this hole that will end up in my armpit.

But I didn't say any of those things. I stared at my shoes while Fen followed Barker down into the darkness and disappeared. What was I going to do, go home?! As a newly minted best friend of mine, you probably already know that was never going to happen. When I was standing on the roof of my house with a golf umbrella over my head hoping for a stiff wind, did I climb down? I did not! It's not in my nature to miss an opportunity to climb into a hole or jump into a rose bush. It just isn't going to happen.

The first thing I realized about the way down was that the ladder we were using was made of metal and it was cold on my hands. And by cold I mean ho-ho-ho polar ice cap cold. These ladder rungs were like popsicles. And according to my internal calendar system, which runs entirely on the number of days before summer break, we were firmly at the hot end of the year. There was only a week of school left and it was warm outside.

"Does anyone else think these ladder rungs are colder than they should be?" I yelled down the tube we had all willingly gotten into. "It's like eighty degrees outside."

"It's science, Jen-Jen," Fen yelled back. "As soon as you go underground the temperature drops like fifty degrees."

"Maybe in Sweden, but I don't think that's right in Nevermind," I said. "Also, my name is Jenny."

"I can see my breath in the headlamp," Barker said. "It's definitely colder than it should be down here. We're in a legitimate survivalist situation."

When Barker Mifflin says we're in survival mode, the smart thing to do is run the other way. He has a sixth sense for this sort of thing. I found the bottom of the ladder and I was standing on a sheet of ice for about one nanosecond and then I was flat on my back.

"It's slippery down here," Fen whispered.

"Thanks for the warning," I said.

"Come on Jenny, we gotta move," Barker said. "It'll keep us warm."

We crawled and slid through a tunnel that was barely big enough to fit through and I kept thinking we were about to stumble into a den of wolverines. Or maybe they were behind me, cutting off the exit, and this would be my final resting place, trapped with two bozos I was dumb enough to follow into a frozen grave.

I heard a banging sound and then the sound of another grate clanging on the concrete floor.

"Okay, I think we're in," Barker said from somewhere ahead of me.

I kept going until I reached the end of the tunnel and then I stood up in a corridor with flickering lights that went to the left and the right.

"Do you feel that?" Barker asked. He was staring at me so the headlamp was in my face. It was like a big, blinding, cyclops eyeball.

"Any chance you could turn that thing off?" I asked.

The light flicked off and there was Barker, holding a piece of paper in his hand.

"Do you feel it?" Barker asked again.

"I'm sorry, what are we supposed to be feeling?" I asked.

"It's not cold anymore."

"Hey you're right!" Fen said. "That's actually kind of weird."

I looked down and realized the floor was no longer icy under my feet.

"Why would they keep a tunnel to the outside so cold?" I asked. "It doesn't make any sense."

"Come on, I've got a map of the place," Barker said, waving the paper he held. "Let's go this way."

We started walking down the corridor as the ceiling lights blinked on and off. The way was narrow, with dull gray walls. Hallways darted off to the left and right, seeping into darkness, full of unknown dangers I could only imagine. If I'm being totally honest, it felt like the kind of place in a movie where bad things happen.

"How'd you get a map of the layout?" Fen asked.

"It's just a rough estimate," Barker said. "I found it on that website I was telling you about. There should be some stairs right around this corner."

Sure enough, there were stairs leading up to a door that was propped open. We made our way up and out of the corridor.

"Whoa," Fen said. "It's huge in here!"

33

It *was* huge, much bigger than I'd expected.

"It's like the old food court," I said. "At the Nevermind Mall. Remember that?"

"I used to get soft pretzels and ice cream there," Barker mumbled, but I could tell his brain was somewhere else. He was taking it all in.

Fun fact: Nevermind did have a mall once, but it closed a few years ago. There's a rumor going around it's infested with zombies who shop for shoes and handbags all day.

"When did the mall close?" Fen asked.

"Two or three years ago," I said. "I think it's full of zombies now."

"Good to know," Fen said.

"This place does look a lot like the old mall," Barker said. "There's this giant open space in the middle, and glassed rooms around the edges, just like a food court."

The glassed rooms were also large, but they were dark inside and far away so we couldn't see inside.

"Let's split up, see what we can find," Barker said. "If you stumble onto anything interesting, yell."

And just like that, Barker Mifflin was gone. He moved fast when he was ready to go, and that left me and Fen Stenson standing at the top of the stairs.

"Wanna stick together?" I asked.

"I was hoping you'd say that."

And so we ventured further inside the Colossal Chemistry building, peeking into rooms and trying light switches that didn't do anything. Some of the rooms were full of examination tables and lots of medical equipment; other rooms had metal desks with computers on them. At some point, I got separated from Fen and found myself standing alone in an orange room with two green tables. There were monitors on the walls and heavy metal drawers with combination locks.

And there was something else.

"What's this thing?" I asked out loud, because

it was such a curious little object. Sitting on the floor, right at the corner of one green table leg, was an orange ball about the size of a marble. The marble-shaped object was covered in a layer of peach fuzz. And it was glowing.

"Hey little buddy," I said.

I bent down and pushed the furry marble with my finger. It rolled a few inches, stopped, and then it glowed and went dark in a slow pattern that felt sad and lonely. *Thrum, thrum, thrum*. I felt bad for the lost little object, so I reached out and picked it up. It felt soft in my hand, like a cotton ball, and it glowed brighter, like it was happy to be picked up.

"Are you lost?" I asked. "You look lost."

The fuzzy marble glowed brighter still, and all at once, it was too hot to hold—like a burning coal from a fire. I screamed and flicked the furry marble out of my hand, and then things got even weirder.

The furry ball crumbled into orange dust and drifted toward the floor.

Barker Mifflin and Fen Stenson arrived, worried because of the scream.

"What's wrong?" Barker asked.

"You okay?" Fen added.

"Yeah, I'm . . . I'm fine. I touched something but it's gone now."

"Touched what?" Barker asked. He seemed a lot more concerned than the situation called for.

"It was nothing, just a fuzzy marble thing. But it disappeared."

"Disappeared?" Fen said. "You mean it rolled away?"

"No I mean I dropped it and then . . . I guess it exploded or something. It's just gone."

And then Barker Mifflin said something that is now ringing in my ears like a siren in my bedroom back home.

"Why is your hand in your armpit?"

CHAPTER 4

TOENAILS

I think it's safe to say we've come to the end of our investigation, wouldn't you agree? The terror in my armpit wasn't caused by a bagel, Fen Stenson, or Bun-Bun eating snuffle sticks.

It was caused by a furry orange marble. Case closed!

I remember everything now. Standing there in the abandoned Colossal Chemistry building, it was like my hand decided it wasn't safe out in the open. It needed protection. It needed a dark place hidden from the rest of the world.

In other words, it needed an armpit! And it turns out mine was the closest one available. This makes me thankful for small victories. Can you imagine if I'd jammed my hand into Fen's armpit? Talk about awkward.

The thing of it is, I don't even remember putting my hand in there. If Barker hadn't told me I was staring at the walls like a numpty with my hand in my armpit, I wouldn't have known it was there at all.

And so, we have some new information! Let's review while I walk to school.

FACT NUMBER ONE: I touched something from an abandoned chemistry lab, it got really hot, and then it exploded into a million pieces. It appears I have ended the life of a furry marble.

FACT NUMBER TWO: something got left on my hand!

FACT NUMBER THREE: whatever was left on my hand decided to hide in my armpit.

FACT NUMBER FOUR: my armpit itches.

And FACT NUMBER FIVE: this is all incredibly embarrassing.

"Hey there, Jen-Jen."

We had arrived at the corner again, the spot where I turn toward the school. Fen rolled up on his scooter, only this time I couldn't hear him coming because Barker Mifflin had fixed the squeak—so of course I made a pancake-face out of myself and nearly jumped into a mailbox.

"Whoa there, Jenster, take it easy," Fen said.

"Don't sneak up on me like that!"

"A thousand apologies. Barker Mifflin really knows how to chill a squeaker. This scooter is purring like a kitten."

"Give me that thing," I said.

I picked up the scooter and threw it into the side of a tree. When Fen got back on, the squeak had returned.

"Much better," I said. "Now listen, I've got something to tell you, but you have to promise not to tell another living soul."

"I can do that," Fen said.

"Are you sure?"

"Nobody keeps a secret like Fen Stenson. My cousin told me he escaped his crib, crawled into the living room, and watched cartoons at midnight. That was nine years ago."

"Wait, he told you this when you were two?"

"Exactly," said Fen. "And I haven't told anyone. You're the first."

"That's a weird secret," I said.

"What secret?"

"You're good."

"You have no idea."

"Okay, before we get separated and go to class ... uh ... well you see ... um ... it's ... uh ..."

"I'm listening."

I took a deep breath and tried not to think about the angry itch under my arm.

"It's possible something followed me out of Colossal Chemistry."

"Go on," Fen said. He was a very good listener.

"It's now living in my armpit."

Fen stayed quiet and stared straight ahead as he kept kicking forward on his scooter, and the wheel squeaked like a chipmunk.

"Well? Are you going to say something?" I asked.

"I once forgot to trim my toenails for seven months," Fen said.

"Ewwwww! That's incredibly totally gross!" I said. "*Seven months?!* How did you even get your feet into your shoes?"

"You'd be surprised how much a toenail will curl up on you," Fen said.

"YUCK!" I yelled. "Why did you tell me that?!"

"I was hoping it would make you feel better. Apparently, I overshot the target."

We were getting close to the front doors of the school, which meant we were almost out of time.

"I guess it does make me feel a *little* better," I said. "I mean, is there anything grosser than curly toenails?"

"It's definitely worse than something living in your armpit," said Fen Stenson, and from that moment on, I knew I could trust him.

"Thank you, Fen."

"You're welcome."

Fen opened the door to the school and I walked into a bustling rotunda filled with kids.

"Meet me at the farthest end of the playground under that big tree during lunch," I said.

"You got it!" Fen said. "And don't worry, I'm sure we can figure out what's going on. How serious could it really be?"

I walked toward my class, and thought, *Yeah, how serious could it really be? It's probably nothing.*

CHAPTER 5

IT GROWS!
(YEAH, IT'S WHAT YOU THINK IT IS)

Now that we've arrived at school, here are three things about my class that are good to know for a newbie like you:

1. Avoid Nadine Burnbaum at all costs. Nadine is known to her many cowering enemies as Naddy Burns. She has a reputation for being mean, nosy, gossipy, and smug, but her real claim to fame is the infamous Naddy Burn. She will

insult you right to your face, then
joyfully say, *You've been burned!*
It's incredibly annoying.
2. Ms. Yang, my teacher, is in her first
    year of teaching. She's enthusiastic,
    fun, and smart. She also has nearly
    no idea what she's doing. Her I like.
3. Due to incredibly bad luck, my seat
    is right next to Naddy Burns. I have
    been burned thousands of times
    this year. Thankfully, I'll be at the
    middle school next year.

I settled into my seat and dropped my backpack on the floor beside me. It was at this point
that I couldn't stand the itch in my armpit for
even one more second without scratching it.

Big mistake.

"I love what you've done with your hair,"
Naddy Burns leaned over and said. "How do
you get it to flow out of your armpits like that?"

"Uh-huh," I mumbled, hoping she'd bother someone else.

A couple of other kids laughed, and then Naddy said, "You've been burned!"

I knew if I ignored Naddy Burns life would be much simpler and easier, but I'd been burned one too many times and this was not the day to burn Jenny!

"Hold still," I said to Naddy. "I'm trying to imagine you with a personality."

Oooooh's erupted all over class because it was rare for anyone to insult Naddy Burns.

"If your brain was dynamite," Naddy said, "there wouldn't be enough to blow your hat off."

Not bad, but I'd been storing up my own insults all school year and I was in no mood.

"Don't worry about me," I said. "Worry about your eyebrows."

The whole class was paying attention now as Ms. Yang struggled with the projector connected to a computer. Technology was not her strong suit.

"If I had a face like yours," Naddy said. "I'd sue my parents."

Okay, that one stung.

I got the feeling Naddy Burns was just getting warmed up, and I was already running out of things to say. I only had one insult left! What had I been thinking?!

"Brush your teeth," I said.

Technically *Brush your teeth* isn't an insult, but I liked how short it was.

Naddy Burns crinkled up her face and seemed to actually think about brushing her teeth. Did I miraculously have her on the ropes?

"You have miles to go before you reach average," Naddy Burns said. "And this conversation is over."

Wait, what just happened? Did Naddy Burns back down?! I'd won! Or at least I'd taken her to a draw, which was practically impossible. Without even thinking, I started scratching my armpit again and that's when I realized whatever was in there wasn't a blotch anymore.

It was a bump.

"You gotta be kidding me," I mumbled.

Ms. Yang finally got the projector working and started a documentary about the Dust Bowl. The lights were turned off and people started whispering and passing notes as the sound of a blistering wind filled the room.

The terror in my armpit grew at an alarming rate while the documentary played. When the show was over and the lights came back up, it was the size of a baseball and it started making weird gurgling sounds. It was squishy, so I could hold it next to my side like a water balloon, squeezing it into something flat enough that no one could see it.

"Do they not feed you at your house?" Naddy Burns said, because of all the gurgling noises coming from my armpit. "Maybe they're hoping you'll run away and join the circus."

Some random kid said, "You've been burned!" But then Naddy Burns gave him an icy stare because he'd stolen her line. At least for the moment, the attention was off me.

I somehow made it through the rest of the morning before the recess bell rang and I ran for the door with my backpack slung over one shoulder. Naddy Burns said something about how I ran like a duck, but I didn't care. I had to get to the tree on the playground, and fast, because the terror in my armpit was getting bigger.

"Fen! Over here!" I yelled when I saw him heading for the tree at a leisurely pace. "Hurry up!"

Fen broke into a run and skidded to a stop on the grassy playground right in front of me.

"How we doin'?" he asked.

"Honestly, I don't think it's going great," I said.

Fen eyeballed my armpit. "It looks about the same. Does it still itch?"

"Nope," I said. "But there's a new problem now."

"A new problem?" Fen asked.

I bent down and set my backpack on the ground and unzipped it. Something was hidden in the backpack, and when I stood up it was hanging from my armpit.

It was about the size of a toaster.

But it looked nothing like a toaster. Describing it is, in fact, terrifying, so I'm putting a pin in that for now.

CHAPTER 6

IT'S STARING AT ME

"Duuuuuuude!" Fen yelled.

"I know," I said. "It's the grossest. And thank you for making me feel even worse."

"What is that thing?!"

"I have no idea!" I said. "And you're not helping!"

For the first time since the terror in my armpit arrived in my life, I felt like crying. I'm pretty sure my chin started to wobble.

"Don't worry Jen-Jen, we're going to figure this out," Fen said. "I promise."

"Are you sure?"

If anyone on planet Earth needed assurance, it was me, but I wasn't that kind of kid. I couldn't even remember the last time I'd asked for help or wished for a compliment. Needing someone's help felt almost as bad as having a creature living in my armpit.

"One hundred percent," Fen said. "Let's not make a mountain out of a molehill. So you've got a . . . a . . . *thing* hanging from your armpit. It's not even that big."

"It's bigger than a bowling ball."

"You're right. That thing is gigantic."

"You don't have to agree with me!"

"You're right again. It's not that big. I doubt anyone would even notice it."

"This is a disaster," I said. I sat down on the grass and covered my face with my hands.

Fen sat down beside me and touched my shoulder, but I shrugged him away. The terror in my armpit groused and grumbled like it was trying to speak.

"This can't possibly get any worse," I said, which I should not have said, because right after I said it the terror in my armpit farted.

"That wasn't me," said Fen. "In case you were wondering."

"This is officially the worst day of my life," I said.

"Hey now, don't say that," said Fen. "All we have to do is figure out how to get that thing off your armpit. Easy peasy."

I peeked out between my fingers so Fen could only see one of my eyes.

"You really think so?" I asked. Inside I was screaming, *You don't need help, Jenny!* Clearly, my voice had other plans.

"Absolutely!" Fen said. "First, we have to make it through the rest of the day. Can you keep this thing in your backpack for a couple more hours?"

I wasn't remotely sure I could do that.

"Maybe?" I answered.

"If anyone can do it, Jen-Jen can!"

"My name is Jenny."

"Okay!"

"You're not going to stop calling me Jen-Jen or Jenster are you?"

"Probably not. But I will be your sidekick until we get this figured out. Meet me right after school and we'll get to work. We got this!"

"If you say so."

The terror in my armpit tried to climb the side of my face, but it slipped and landed in my backpack.

"This is getting super awkward," I said.

Okay, enough procrastinating. Now is about as good a time as any to tell you what the terror in my armpit looks like. I've waited this long, but you're going to find out eventually. Will we still be friends after this? I give it a fifty-fifty chance.

Here are four details I think you should know:

1. The terror in my armpit is orange and fuzzy.
2. So far, it's sprouted seven ghastly limbs of various sizes. They're like dangly rubber bands that shoot out in every direction and, apparently, help it climb the side of my face.
3. It has one hideous eyeball and it's not small. It's about the size of a tennis ball, it's furry, and it's staring at me.
4. So far it doesn't seem to have a mouth, but that could change. It does have four or five horrible holes that randomly open and close. *Is it breathing?*

The terror in my armpit is obviously turning into some sort of monster, and it's getting heavy.

It helps to keep it in my backpack so the weight rests in there instead of pulling on my armpit. Which brings up another detail I should probably tell you. The one-eyed menace in my backpack is hanging from something that's gotten thicker and longer and stretchier. I basically have a bungee cord stuck to my armpit, with a horrible orange blob stuck to the other end.

So, yeah, I'm having a totally normal day.

Luckily, I'm a self-sufficient go-getter who jumps over garbage cans and hurls insults at Naddy Burns. I can handle this. And I have Fen Stenson to help me, but I'm going to be honest: I need to avoid Barker Mifflin at all costs. I'm 100 percent sure Barker's solution to this problem would be immediate removal by force, and I can't even begin to imagine him pulling on the bungee cord in my armpit like a tug of war. I just can't.

Nope, at least until I get home, I'm hiding this thing in my backpack.

CHAPTER 7

YOU'VE BEEN BURNED!

I made it to the end of the school day without anyone discovering the terror in my armpit. I know what you're thinking. *How did my super good friend Jenny accomplish this amazing outcome?*

Let's just say I got lucky. After recess, Ms. Yang decided to cash in her one and only Library Bonanza Ticket. What is a Library Bonanza Ticket, you ask? It's pretty much exactly what it sounds like. I know because I've seen the tickets when the school librarian, Mr. Glarfman, hands them out. Each teacher gets one for the year, and they allow a class to take over the library for an extended visit. And by extended, I mean the rest of the school day.

Ms. Yang said with only a few days of school left before summer break, she wanted to give us two full hours of library free time to test out books we might like to read over the summer. It was perfect because I found a quiet corner all by myself to read books while the terror in my armpit made increasingly weird noises in my backpack.

As soon as the bell rang, I ran for the exits without talking to a single person and burst out of the school doors into a sunny afternoon. The birds were singing, the sun was shining, and Fen Stenson was dutifully waiting for me with one foot on his scooter.

"Let's roll!" I said as I ran past him toward my house.

"Rollin'!" Fen replied, kicking his scooter into gear and chasing after me.

Part of why I was moving like the wind was because the terror in my armpit had gotten bigger while I sat reading books in the library. My backpack was stretched to the point where the zipper was ready to snap right off.

I stopped running so I could catch my breath. "I'm gonna need you to hop off that scooter," I gasped to Fen as he pulled up next to me. "I'm totally bonked."

"Bonked?" Fen asked, stepping to the side so I could drop the backpack onto his scooter.

"Out of energy, hitting the wall, tired of carrying a large and heavy orange blob on my back . . . You know, bonked."

"Got it," Fen said as he looked at the backpack with some alarm. "Is that thing getting bigger? How's your armpit doing?"

I thought about how to answer. All I knew for certain was that the bungee cord or hose or whatever it was connecting my armpit to the thing in the backpack had grown longer and stretchier. It had to be three feet long at this point.

"As long as I don't get too far away from it, the ol' armpit is doing fine," I said. "Let's get to the house before—"

"Well, well, well, if it isn't Tweedle Dee and Tweedle Dork."

Ugh. Naddy Burns had decided to drop by and taunt us. Of course she had. I gotta hand it to her; she has perfect timing when it comes to spreading misery. She sneered as she rode up on her fancy bicycle.

"We're just passing through," Fen said. "Nothing to see here."

Naddy snickered. "I'll say. *Definitely* nothing to see here."

"Something I can help you with, Naddy?" I asked as politely as I could. "We really do have to be going."

The backpack wobbled on the scooter and made some squishy noises.

Luckily, she didn't seem to notice. "I saw you run out of the library when school was over," she said. "What's the rush? Gotta get home before you turn into a pumpkin?"

I fake laughed, hoping it would make her go away. "You got me there."

"Come on, Jen-Jen," Fen said. "Let's motor."

Naddy stared Fen up and down. "Last time I saw a face like yours was at the zoo. I fed it a banana."

Fen looked confused. "They let you feed animals at the zoo here?" Fen asked. "Cool. That's not a thing in Sweden. I'm from Sweden."

Now Naddy looked confused. But she quickly regained her composure. "You've been buuuur-rrrrrrned!" she howled and then she threw her head back and laughed straight up into the sky.

"She is really annoying," Fen said.

"You have no idea."

Naddy's head snapped forward. She stared darts into our faces.

"Something's going on with you two and I'm going to figure out what it is," Naddy said. "You're not smart enough to hide it for long."

"Okay, bye then," I said, and Naddy rode off on her bike looking for someone else to torment.

"Why are you on Naddy's radar?" Fen asked.

"I might have gotten into an insult contest with her earlier today."

"Are you sure that was a good idea?" Fen asked.

"In hindsight, I can see how it wasn't great timing."

The backpack lolled back and forth and fell off the scooter with a sloshy sound like grimy water glugging out of a garbage can. Then the zipper made a pop sound and a glob of orange fur poked out.

"Run!" I yelled. I picked up the backpack in a bear hug and broke into a sprint.

One of the limbs popped out of the backpack and wobbled around in the air and then the top of the backpack burst open and the giant furry eyeball stared up at me.

"Open the door!" I yelled.

We were at my house and Fen rode past me, threw open the door, and jumped out of the way.

"Coming through!" I screamed as the rest of the terror in my armpit started oozing out of the backpack like a giant glob of nacho cheese sauce.

I ran through the door and there was my dad, standing in the kitchen eating a bowl of cereal.

"Hey, kiddo, how was sch—"

"Heading upstairs to play video games with Fen!" I didn't even break stride. I just kept running right up the stairs.

"Who's Fen?" my dad said.

I took two steps at a time up the stairs and didn't look back. When I reached my room. I flung the door open, threw the backpack onto my bed, and closed the door behind me.

"That was a close call," I said, but Fen didn't respond. "Fen?"

I looked around my room and realized I'd lost Fen somewhere in my house.

I opened my door and peeked out into the hall, but he wasn't there. Then I heard voices drifting up from the first floor. After that, I heard laughter. I frowned. Holding my breath, I tiptoed to the top of the stairs, stretching my armpit hose to the limit.

"I'd go Fruit Loops a distant third," Fen was saying. "Cinnamon Toast Crunch a close second, and Golden Grahams top of the heap."

"I'm a Frosted Mini-Wheats man myself," my dad replied. "Very filling."

"I can respect that," Fen said.

"Hey dad!" I yelled. "Sorry, had to use the bathroom! Is it okay if Fen and I hang out and play video games until mom gets home?"

There was a pause, then my dad appeared at the bottom of the stairs. He was still in his pajamas. In one hand he held a bowl of cereal. In the other he held a spoon. I felt a tug at my armpit hose, but I held my ground.

"No homework?" he asked.

"It's the last week of school," I said, trying to act cool and calm. "Ms. Yang let us watch a documentary and then we went to the library. When's dinner?"

"Six thirty would be my guess. I'm on a deadline, so find me in my office if you need me."

Under normal circumstances, I might have asked: *If you're on a deadline, then why are you eating cereal in the middle of the afternoon?* But I forced a smile instead.

"Cool!" I said enthusiastically. "Enjoy that deadline. I'll meet you for dinner."

My dad looked puzzled. "You okay? Want me to bring you a snack?"

"No!" I half yelled. "I mean, no thank you— they gave us cupcakes at the end of the day. End-of-school-year stuff."

My dad nodded and shoved a spoonful of cereal in his mouth.

Fen raced out of the kitchen. "Nice to meet

you, Mr. Kim," he said, hurrying past my dad up the stairs. "Let's play video games!"

I had to give Fen credit; he was really selling the video game thing.

My dad wandered toward his office. Fen followed me as I darted back into my room and silently closed the door behind us.

"Oh, wow," Fen said.

I didn't really want to know what Fen was saying *oh, wow* about. I'd already had plenty of *wow* moments earlier in the day.

"Come on, Jenny," I whispered to myself as I stared at the floor. "Buck up, you can do this."

I gulped one more big breath of air and exhaled, then raised my eyes toward my backpack.

I wished I hadn't.

The cord running from my armpit had grown to at least nine feet long. It was twisted and tangled in a heap on the bed. And the thing attached to the other end? It was bigger than a bean bag chair.

CHAPTER 8

SNERB!

"Probably better if we don't move," I said.

We were both still standing in front of the door, eyes locked on the far corner of my room.

"How many arms does it have?" asked Fen. "Or are they legs? Or . . . *limbs?*"

"No fingers or thumbs, just a bizarro suction cup at the end," I said. "They look like vacuum cleaner hoses."

"Okay so they're hoses," Fen said. "And I'm counting twelve of them."

I wasn't sure about the arms. What I did know

was that the orange furry blob had no bones, because it had spread out across my bed like a puddle of pudding. It lay there, flapping its hoses around like it was trying to feel things. They looked like those inflatable tube men at used car lots that rise and fall in crazy directions. The fuzzy eyeball had expanded to the size of a frying pan, and it was trying to look at the entire world at one time, darting back and forth and up and down.

"Unfortunately, we can't cut it off your armpit," Fen said.

"Sure we can," I said, suddenly very interested in this idea. "I could just take a pair of scissors and snip, snip—problem solved."

"You're not going to want to do that," Fen said. He was acting like he knew something I didn't know, which was alarming given that Fen Stenson is probably the most clueless kid I know.

"Fen, what are you not telling me?"

"You're going to want to sit down for this," Fen said.

Uh-oh. I slid down with my back against the door until my butt hit the floor. My mind was racing. Was Fen somehow responsible for what was going on? Had he smuggled in some awful creature from Sweden that never should have left Scandinavia?

"Tell me. What's going on?"

The table lamp by my bed crashed into the floor and then the clock fell off the wall.

"Those hose arms are going to destroy my room," I muttered.

"Hang on," Fen said. "I have an idea." He pulled out his phone and did some tapping on the screen and a lo-fi hip-hop beat started playing.

"Sleepy music," I said. "Good call."

The hose limbs started to deflate, the giant eyeball drooped, and then the disgusting thing sitting on my bed started snoring. It sounded like an elephant trunk slurping dirty lake water, but at least it wasn't destroying my room anymore.

Fen offered a shaky smile.

"Why can't we cut this thing off my armpit, Fen? Tell me!"

Fen dug into his own backpack and pulled out a folder.

"When we were at Colossal Chemistry and we got separated, I found the director's office. She left some papers behind . . . in the desk."

"Seems like she would have taken those," I said. "Or at least locked the desk."

"I'm getting the feeling there were only a few people in the building at the end," Fen explained. "I think those last few people, including the director, had to leave in a hurry. Anyway, the desk *was* locked, I'm just really good at lock picking. It's a hobby of mine."

My eyes narrowed. "You pick locks? As a hobby?"

"I also knit," Fen said. He put the folder down, dug into his backpack again, and pulled out a square of knitted fabric. "I made you a potholder."

"I feel like we're getting off the subject," I said. "But thank you. You are aware I don't cook?"

He blinked, "It doubles as a seat cushion."

"About this folder you found?" I pressed. Keeping Fen Stenson on task was more challenging than winning the insult battle with Naddy Burns.

"Right." He nudged the folder across the floor of my room toward me like it was radioactive. The folder was orange, with the words "Colossal Chemistry Dev Log" printed in green stencil. Someone had written a number seven under the title.

"There were a bunch of these log files locked in the desk drawer, but I took them all and crammed them into one folder," Fen said. "And then I spent all afternoon at school reading them."

The fuzzy orange blob on my bed made a gloppy, goopy sound and then it expanded another foot in diameter.

"It's growing again," Fen observed.

"Stay on task, Fen. What was in the logs you're not telling me?"

"Oh, a lot of stuff was in there," Fen said. "Took me two hours to read it all."

"And?"

Fen leaned forward and opened the folder. I saw that he had written down some notes with a red pen. In my experience, red ink is never a good thing. Was I going to be stuck with the terror in my armpit for the rest of my life?

"First of all, Colossal Chemistry was doing top secret research on some sort of pollution-eating organism," he said, "Which, I have to say, is really cool."

"Wait—this thing they were making, it *ate* pollution?"

"Exactly. Right out of the air," Fen added. "They had quite a few complications though."

"Like what?"

"Mainly that the pollution-eating organisms got too big."

I braced myself and asked an all-important question.

"How big?"

"The logs didn't say how big, but it did say some other interesting stuff."

"Like?"

"Remember how it was really cold when we went down that tunnel? That's because these things hate cold air. They won't go anywhere near it."

"So Colossal Chemistry kept all the exits freezing cold to keep these things from escaping?"

Fen nodded. "And they developed some sort of storage for them when they got to a certain size, but it's unclear what it was. A lot of the stuff in the log was redaction city."

"You mean lots of parts were scratched out so you couldn't read them?"

"Exactly. We're getting to the not-so-great stuff I found in the log."

"Hit me," I said. "I can take it."

"Humans should not make direct contact with one of them, because the human will become a host creature."

I gasped. "I'm a host creature?!"

"I think that furry little marble you touched when we were sneaking around in the old building was a pollution eating organism."

"Yeah, I'm getting that," I said. Without thinking I scratched my armpit and the entire hose connecting me to the thing on my bed lit up from inside with an orange glow. The giant eyeball fluttered, but then closed again.

"And this is really important, Jen-Jen," Fen said. "You can't cut it off. If you do it will make that thing very angry and it will start eating cars and trees and mailboxes and then it will eat the two of us. Actually it will eat us first, then the other stuff."

"What?!"

"It will eat us," Fen said. "For dinner."

"Is there any good news in that dumb folder or is it *all* bad?!"

"There is this one interesting part that's not technically bad," Fen said.

"Tell me," I said.

"There was a naming party where they tried to name the organisms," Fen said. "Some of the options they considered were Boss Hog, Spam Popsicle, and Flying Spaghetti Monster."

"Those are terrible names," I said.

"They also thought about using Frankensteinberger, Gene Simmons, and NomNomNom."

"I kind of like NomNomNom. That's not bad."

"They settled on Snerb for no particular reason," Fen said. "So at least we know what happened. You've been Snerbed."

"Snerbed?!" I whined. "But I don't want to be Snerbed!"

"Yours is a heavy burden to bear, Jenster,"

Fen said. "But if you ever decide to learn how to cook, you do have a fancy potholder, so there's that."

I imagined myself much older, standing in the kitchen happily cooking as the Snerb set out potholders on the table and the two of us ate casseroles and watched game shows on television.

"What are we going to do, Fen?"

Fen dug into his backpack and pulled out a tablet, then sat on the floor of my room cross-legged like we were in first grade and our teacher was about to start story time.

He tapped the screen a few times then looked up.

"We can't figure this out alone and we have to move fast. We're going to need more help."

I wasn't even comfortable with the help I was already getting, but desperate times called for desperate measures.

"Help from who?" I asked.

A few more taps on the screen and then Fen

turned the tablet toward me. A woman in a white coat was staring at me. The lab coat had a Colossal Chemistry logo on it. She was tall, with a thin face and a long nose. She wore horn rimmed glasses and a tight bun of blond hair. Her mood seemed grim.

"Who is she?" I asked.

Fen turned the tablet back toward himself and tapped a few more times on the screen.

"She's the help we're looking for."

CHAPTER 9

ONLY THE ROBOT KNOWS DANGER!

I had my doubts about anyone from Colossal Chemistry helping us, even if we were lucky enough to find them, but what else was I going to do? The terror in my armpit didn't even come close to fitting in my armpit anymore. For all I knew it was only going to get bigger. I sat at my desk and flipped open my laptop while Fen kept tapping away on his tablet.

"The name on her lab coat is Vexler," I said. "Maybe we can find something online about her."

"Actually her full name is Dr. Vernsy Von Vexler."

"That can't be a real name," I said. "How do you even know that?"

"Because I was in her office at Colossal Chemistry," Fen said, and then he picked up the file. "These were her notes, and I think she left them there for someone to find."

"You think she went rogue?" I asked.

"I don't know," Fen said shaking his head. "Maybe? And if she did, she might know how to help us."

"Where did you find the picture of her?" I asked.

"Some biochemistry convention where she was scheduled to speak. Her talk was called 'Beware the Coming Storm.' And her title? *Former* head of research at Colossal Chemistry. I think she may have been trying to warn people about what was going on in there."

"Are there notes about her talk?" I asked.

"Maybe there's something about removing a monster from your armpit."

"That's the thing," Fen said. "She didn't give the talk. She never showed up."

"That's weird."

"I think she was going to share stuff she wasn't supposed to," Fen said. "And someone at Colossal Chemistry stepped in."

I looked at Fen and thought about what this could mean.

"You think she was *silenced*?" I asked.

Fen shrugged again. "Or something worse."

The thing from my armpit made some bubbling sounds and lolled back and forth on my bed. Was it growing or just sleeping?

"Let me see the file," I said.

Fen handed it over and I flipped through the pages. I thought there might be a clue that would help me. There were charts and equations that didn't make any sense, and dense paragraphs full of words and terms I didn't understand—like "chromatography" and "molecular weight."

"What's this line of nonsense at the bottom of the last page?" I asked.

Fen glanced over and shook his head, frowned. He had no idea.

The line read: ONLY THE ROBOT KNOWS ACHTUNG.

Maybe it was some sort of secret code—a message, meant only for someone who knew how to read it. Maybe I could be that someone.

"Okay, Fen," I said. "Time for some computer investigating work. Are you with me?"

"I'm at a dead end," Fen said. "Whatcha got?"

I stood up and started pacing my room. There was something about robots that was important, but I couldn't remember what it was.

"My dad is a computer programmer," I said. "He likes to show me popular websites and then open up the code. Like he's a mechanic opening up the hood of a car so he can dig around in there. I usually don't pay any attention, but the other day he wanted to tell me something about robots. I just can't remember what it was."

"Robots are taking over the world," Fen said. "That's happening."

"Go to one of those translation sites and put in "a*chtung*." I think that's German or something close."

Fen got busy and I kept pacing. *Only the robot knows* . . . The robot knows *what* though?

"Okay I got it," Fen said. "You were right, it's German."

"German for what?"

"*Achtung* means danger," Fen said.

Now we were getting somewhere. I mumbled the complete sentence so I could hear it out loud.

"Only the robot knows danger."

I felt like I was right around the corner from solving a puzzle, like the solution was on the tip of my tongue but I couldn't quite remember it.

And then my phone rang. Unfortunately, I had my ringer set to play a classic 80s hair metal song because the only people who ever called me were my parents.

"Uh-oh," Fen said.

The sound of my phone woke up the terror that used to be in my armpit. All the hose arms started waving around the room banging into things and the giant eyeball opened up like a garage door. The eyeball darted around in every direction searching for the sound and then it locked on my phone, which unfortunately was also in my hand.

"Something about that thing has changed," I said, and boy, was I right.

All at once it sounded like a dozen vacuum cleaners half-clogged with cream of mushroom soup. It was a slurpy, gloppy, air-filled noise filling the entire room.

"The hose arms are sucking in air!" Fen yelled.

Wind was whipping around my room like a tornado.

"And the holes in the side of the furry orange blob are sending the air back into the room!" I yelled.

Before I tell you what else was happening in my room, I want to thank you again for being my friend through thick and thin. I mean let's be honest, when you met me, I had a little red blotch in my armpit. It was no big deal. I probably seemed like a normal kid. You probably thought we would go on bike rides and play board games together. It would be fun! And you've stuck with me as the little red blotch outgrew my armpit, outgrew my backpack, and took over my bedroom. But now, since I really am a good friend, I feel like it's only fair to tell you . . .

I think I may have completely lost control of this situation. You may not want to hang around while some sort of vacuum cleaner monster tears my room apart.

"What's it doing?!" Fen yelled. Fen's scooter was inching toward my bed near one of the vacuum hose arms, but that was the least of my problems. My *arm* was being pulled toward the bed! This was terrifying because the various hoses were sucking up all kinds of stuff in my room including my stapler, my book report, and my headphones.

The terror that came from my armpit was vacuuming up my whole room.

I let go of my phone as it was still ringing, and it flew across the open space between me and the Snerb and into a vacuum hose.

"It ate my phone!" I yelled.

"It's trying to eat my scooter!" Fen replied, and he was right. It was trying to swallow the scooter whole, but the scooter was jackknifed at the hose opening like a wishbone at a Thanksgiving dinner.

My pillow went next with a *flump* sound as it hit the end of a hose. After that it was like a snake eating a chicken egg as the pillow moved slowly closer to the furry orange blob and then finally *thwomp!* The shape of my pillow disappeared right into the Snerb. But all the objects the Snerb was eating weren't even half the problem.

It was spitting most of that stuff back out!

"Incoming!" I yelled.

The stapler flew out of an air hole, hit the wall, bounced off the ceiling, and nearly clobbered Fen in the face. My homework blasted back into the room in a flurry of paper and then the Snerb expanded like a balloon, made a giant *fawump* sound, and my pillow reentered the atmosphere in the form of a million tiny feathers. The wind was whipping and the feathers created a whiteout right there in my bedroom.

"I can't see anything!" I yelled. "It's like a blizzard in here!"

Sticky, wet feathers pelted me across the face and stuck in my hair and I'm pretty sure at least three went right down my throat. Note to self: shut your pie hole when you're caught in a feather storm.

Just as quickly as the Snerb had gone into overdrive, everything went deadly quiet. The hoses stopped sucking and a million feathers slowly settled onto the floor of my room.

"Um, Jen-Jen?"

"Yeah, Fen?"

"I'm having a little trouble over here."

I wiped the feathers from my face, coughed up a feather ball, and turned toward Fen. Unfortunately I responded by screaming. You would have too. One of the tubes was examining Fen's face like an elephant trunk searching for peanuts.

"I really don't want to end up inside a Snerb," Fen whispered. "Can you hit it with a baseball bat or a golf club?"

I didn't have a baseball bat or a golf club, but I did know some sweet wrestling moves (they were pretty much the only things my brothers ever taught me). I raised my arms up in the air, got ready to attack, and then the hose retracted back to the bed, satisfied that eating Fen would be a terrible idea.

"Whew," Fen said. "That was a close one."

I heard a *fwomp* sound from behind me and my phone bounced across the floor and landed at my feet. The one giant eyeball was staring at me from the bed.

"There is a small item of good news in all of this," I said as I looked at the disaster that used to be my bedroom.

"And that is?" Fen asked.

"I know what the message meant."

"What message?"

"*Only the robot knows danger*, remember? The message Vexler left behind," I said. "I know what it means."

I looked at my phone screen and saw that it was Barker Mifflin who had called. I needed to call him back, but it would have to wait.

"Maybe turn the ringer off on that thing," Fen said. "Clearly, Snerbs don't like loud music."

I flipped the ringer off and sat down next to Fen.

"Can I borrow your tablet?" I asked.

"What for?" Fen asked. But he didn't wait for an answer. He handed it over and I started tapping commands on the screen.

"We're going to figure out what the robot knows."

CHAPTER 10

DOCTOR VERNSY VON VEXLER

Like I said before, my dad is always trying to show me technology tricks and, usually, I only half listen to him. Okay, let's be real, I never listen to any of that stuff. I just nod and smile, but it turns out some of those tidbits have found their way into my brain anyway.

"I remember my dad explaining how you could find hidden web pages on the internet," I said. "Like things someone would put on their site that weren't for just anyone. The trick was figuring out how to make that stuff visible."

"I almost got eaten by a Snerb," Fen said.

"Earth to Fen!" I said. "This is important."

"Right," Fen said. "Hidden pages?"

"When a search engine goes out looking for pages, it doesn't find everything."

"It's unnerving when it stares at me," Fen said.

I glanced at the Snerb and sure enough, its one giant eyeball was watching us.

"Anyway, when someone doesn't want a search engine to find a page, they hide it with a tag called robot.txt."

"That's actually kind of interesting," Fen said. "I think I'm starting to see where you're going."

"I bet if we go to the Colossal Chemistry website, but add atchtung.robot.txt, we'll find something."

I found the old Colossal Chemistry website,

which was ColossalChem.com, and added the extra line: ColossalChem.com/achtung.robot.txt

"Is that what I think it is?" Fen asked, leaning in so close his face practically glowed off the tablet screen.

"You're fogging up the glass," I said.

"Sorry, backing up," Fen said.

"It's a chat feature," I said.

The chat feature was staring back at us right there in the middle of the screen. A *hidden* chat feature, left there by Vexler herself.

I read the headline on the chat box: "For emergency use only."

"I'd say we're having a serious emergency, wouldn't you?" Fen asked.

I nodded and put my fingers over the keys on the tablet.

"What should I say?" I asked.

"Here, I'll do it," Fen said. "I got a B- on my last paper. I can write."

Fen started typing into the chat box:

My best friend Jen-Jen
touched a furry round
ball at Colossal Chemistry,
then she wiped her hand
in her armpit.

"I'm not sure we need to tell her about my armpit," I said. "I mean—"

Fen hit SEND.

"Hey!" I said.

"That was definitely a B+ message," Fen said. "Maybe even an A-."

"I did like the best friend part," I admitted. "You really think so?"

It did sort of seem like the day we were having was forging a special bond between us. I liked Fen. He was fun even when something that grew out of my armpit was trying to eat his scooter.

"I'm the new kid in town," Fen mumbled, shrugging his shoulders. "And you've been nice to me since day one. And I know your name is

Jenny, I just like Jen-Jen better. Or Jenster."

"I've never had a nickname before," I said, and it was true, I hadn't. "It's cool."

We both heard a soft ding sound coming from the tablet.

"She responded!" We both yelled at the same time. The Snerb made some wheezing sounds, coughed up about a hundred pillow feathers, and stared at us.

"Shhhhh," I whispered.

And then we started to type, back and forth, for the next few minutes.

The following is the full list of chat messages between yours truly and a scientist called Vexler:

Vexler:

Who is this?!

Me and Fen:

This is Fen and Jenny.

Who are you?

Vexler:

Doctor Vernsy Von Vexler.
How did you get into the
Colossal Chemistry building?

Me and Fen:

We went in through
a tunnel. It was cold
in there.

Vexler:

Well, sure it was cold
in there! Otherwise
the Snerbs would
have escaped.

Me and Fen:

We have a Snerb stuck
to Jenny's armpit. Are
you saying we should
freeze it?

Vexler:

Too late for that.
How big is it?

Me and Fen:

Bigger than a bean
bag chair but smaller
than a car.

Vexler:

Bigger than a bean bag
chair?! Why didn't you
contact me sooner?!

Me and Fen:

We only just found
this chat feature.
Sorry.

Vexler:

This is a serious situation.

Me and Fen:

We figured that part out on our own.

Vexler:

What a disaster.

Me and Fen:

So far, we're not feeling like this chat feature is very helpful.

Vexler:

Hold, please.

"Did she just put us on hold?" I asked.

"It would appear so," Fen said.

About a minute later, Vexler was back.

Vexler:

> Meet me here in exactly
> 36 minutes.
> 46.05632400512695,
> -118.31214904785156

Me and Fen:

> Did we mention we're
> not scientists? And
> we're eleven years old.
> We don't know what
> those numbers are for.

Vexler:

> They're GPS coordinates,
> you nitwits! Be there in
> 36 minutes or you're on
> your own. And bring the
> Snerb! We've got some
> work to do.

Me and Fen:

We can't exactly leave the Snerb in Jenny's room, anyway. It's attached to her armpit.

Me and Fen:

Would you happen to know if we can remove the Snerb from the armpit?

Me and Fen:

Hello?

Vexler never answered our last three messages, so we figured she was on her way to wherever we were going.

"Any idea how to find an address with those numbers?" I asked Fen.

"None whatsoever," Fen said. "But we have a

mutual friend who's also a survivalist in training. I bet this would be a cakewalk for him."

"Barker Mifflin," I said.

I wasn't sure about calling Barker. Not only was he a survivalist in training, but he was also sort of intense. Plus, I still felt like maybe I didn't need any more help, since I had rarely asked for help in the past. Was I really going to ask *another* person for help?

"I know what you're thinking," Fen said.

"I'll bet you five thousand feathers you don't," I replied.

"You don't like asking for help," Fen said as he reached over and picked a feather off my forehead. "But Jenny, sometimes we all need help. Next time it'll be me. It's nothing to feel bad about."

I thought about what Fen said and I agreed, but that didn't make it any easier to admit I needed friends to help me.

"Fine," I said. "I owe you five thousand feathers."

I dialed up Barker, put the phone on speaker mode so Fen and I could both talk, and Barker answered on the first ring.

"I didn't see you after school," Barker said. "How's the situation with the armpit?"

So embarrassing.

"It's complicated," I said.

"Complicated how?" Barker asked.

"Um . . . how can I say this so you won't freak out," I replied.

"Something is growing out of Jen-Jen's armpit," Fen said.

"Thanks a lot, Fen!"

Total silence on the other end of the line.

"Barker?" I said. "Anyone there?"

"Are we talking about a potential zombie-land event or what?"

"No, not that, it's not a zombie. It's a Snerb."

"Listen, Barker, we're in a little bit of a rush on this," Fen said. "Could we text you some GPS coordinates and have you send us an actual address? We don't know how to read the numbers."

"Kid's stuff," Barker said. "Send them over. Are you meeting someone there?"

I whispered to Fen. "I'm not sure we should tell him we're meeting Vexler there."

"I agree," Fen whispered back. "Or maybe he could be good to have around?"

"You do realize I can hear everything you're saying?" Barker said. "You two would make lousy international spies. Why does this sort of thing always happen to unprepared door-knobs?"

"Did he just call us doorknobs?" Fen asked.

"He might be right," I said.

"Point taken," Fen agreed.

"Okay we'll meet you there," I said. "And bring all that survivalist stuff you carry around. We might need it."

"Holding for coordinates," Barker said, and then he hung up.

"That kid was made for the moment," Fen said.

"I know, right?"

I texted the GPS coordinates to Barker's phone and then we sat there for a second staring at the Snerb. My room was basically destroyed, and we needed to get a very large Snerb down the stairs—and who knew how far after that! This was going to be a challenge.

"I'm going to need you to go to the garage," I said.

"What for?" Fen asked.

I took a deep breath and stood up slowly so I wouldn't spook the thing stuck to my armpit.

"We're gonna need a wheelbarrow, a tarp, and some bungee cords."

CHAPTER 11

THE AMAZING WHEELBARROW BELLY FLOP

While Fen Stenson was searching my family garage for supplies, I stood in my room contemplating my next move. The way I figured it, there were three things I had to accomplish in the next few minutes:

1. Keep the Snerb as calm as possible.
2. Get the Snerb to trust me.
3. Push the Snerb down a flight of stairs.

For the first task, I decided I would keep the Snerb as calm as possible by talking to it in a tranquil voice.

"Hey there," I said quietly. "I'm sorry I don't have anything very good to eat in my room. I'm sure the stapler and my homework and my pillow were a big letdown."

The Snerb blinked but didn't move, so I moved on to task number two: get the Snerb to trust me.

"Hey, I have an idea," I said. "We could go outside and see if there's something better to eat in the front yard. I'm sure we can find something and I know just where to go. You can trust ol' Jenny, I'm a real pro at finding garbage."

The giant Snerb eyeball widened like it was excited.

"How's about you start by rolling off my bed onto the floor?" I said. "Then I'll show you how to get to the front yard. It's not even that far away!"

I tried to make it sound like a fabulous adventure that would end with something the Snerb would want to eat, even though I had no idea what it would want. Would it eat the yard? Would it eat my dad's car? Then I pointed to the floor and hoped it would understand I wanted it to get off my bed.

The Snerb made some burbling sounds, then it purred like a giant cat. It wobbled like a massive pile of orange Jell-O, but it stayed firmly planted on the bed.

Then something occurred to me that I hadn't thought of before. I wondered, was the Snerb like a dog—a super-smart alien dog—and the tube connected to my armpit like a leash? Maybe the Snerb saw me as its owner and it would follow if I led.

"I'm just going to open my bedroom door and walk out into the hallway," I said. "Come on, you can do it. We're going for a walk."

I opened my door and walked right out until

the hose connecting me to the terror that came from my armpit tightened. It stopped me in my tracks and the Snerb made a fart sound.

"You can trust me," I said calmly. "And I'm your owner, so you have to come with me."

I tugged on the hose attached to my armpit and the Snerb flopped forward. It glopped down the side of my bed like a wet ball of slime, its hose arms flailing in every direction as the eyeball rolled out of view. The eyeball was staring at the floor, but then the eyeball floated through the middle of the blob and popped out on the side. The eyeball opened up again, blinked, and stared at me like an obedient puppy.

"What a neat trick!" I said, trying to encourage the Snerb as I also tried not to throw up. I mean, come on! Wouldn't you want to barf? An eyeball the size of a frying pan had just traveled right through the middle of its body and popped out on the other side. That's just wrong.

I turned and inched toward the top of the

stairs. I paused just as the front door burst open and Fen ran through pushing a wheelbarrow.

"Line it up right at the bottom of the stairs," I said as calmly as I could. "And get ready to throw a tarp over this thing fast."

I turned back to the Snerb. It was trying to eat my desk with one of its hoses.

"Let's not eat my desk," I said, and the hose let go. It appeared I had accomplished task number two on my list: get the Snerb to trust me!

"Come on, we're headed for the front yard!" I said excitedly.

I moved forward a few feet, heading down the hallway, and the Snerb reached my bedroom door. It had to squeeze through and use its hose arms to pull and push, then it plopped out on the other side and stood in front of the stairs.

I thought about the third task I had planned to accomplish: push the Snerb down the stairs.

This was starting to feel like a task that didn't make any sense. I had gained its trust, and if I pushed it down the stairs, it wasn't going to trust me anymore.

I forced myself to smile at it. "So listen," I murmured gently. "This next part might seem a little scary, but it's actually a lot of fun. We do it all the time. It's called falling down the stairs."

The big eyeball darted nervously back and forth between the stairs and the hallway.

"Come on down!" Fen yelled up the stairs. "I'll catch you in this wheelbarrow!"

The Snerb started lolling back toward the bedroom door, but I got behind it and gave it a good hard shove. Its body was furry on the outside, squishy on the inside, so it rolled like a flat tire on a monster truck. The Snerb started making squishy noises, then its hoses started dancing in the air searching for something to hold onto. But it was too late. One more big push and it tumbled down the stairs, end over end, burping and glopping all the way to the bottom.

When it was about halfway down, I remembered I was attached to the giant furry blob currently falling down the stairs, and it yanked on my armpit and pulled me right down with it. Somehow, I managed to stay on my feet, but I was moving at a sprint until I reached the last few steps, tripped over my own feet, and went into a belly flop.

"Coming in hot!" I yelled.

The Snerb crashed into the wheelbarrow, then I splashed into the Snerb like it was a kiddie pool full of water. The terror that came from my armpit did a very nice job of breaking my fall, and I found myself lying face down on a carpet of fur, staring at an eyeball bigger than my head.

"You did so good!" I praised. "You fell down a flight of stairs like a real pro! Plus you broke my fall. You might have just saved my life!"

Against all odds, the Snerb seemed genuinely happy to have fallen down the stairs, waving it's noodle arms softly and glowing bright orange.

I climbed off the wheelbarrow and stood next to Fen.

"You've got a little bit of Snerb on your face," he said.

I brushed a goopy, fuzzy clump of Snerb off my chin.

"We gotta get out of here fast," I said. "Before my dad wanders in."

"The tarp and the bungee cords are outside," Fen said. "To the yard!"

And with that, Fen Stenson picked up the wheelbarrow handles, did a three-point turn in the landing area, and rolled a sloshing load of Snerb out the front door.

CHAPTER 12

NATTY BURNS RETURNS!

Fen and I threw the tarp over the wheelbarrow and strapped it down with bungee cords so the only thing anyone would be able to see was a hose coming from under my arm.

"How am I going to hide this hideous extra limb coming out of my armpit?" I asked Fen. It looked like a third arm covered in orange fur.

Fen darted over by the front door and came back holding a bag. "I was thinking the same thing when I was getting all this stuff in the garage. How about this?"

Fen was holding an orange plastic rain poncho.

"Same color as the Snerb and everything," Fen said. "What a score."

"But it's not raining!" I complained. "Why would I be wearing a rain poncho?"

"Because the Jenster is always prepared for bad weather," Fen said. "Just go with it."

I rolled my eyes and one of the vacuum hose arms slid out from under the tarp and flopped on the front yard.

"Can you fix that?" I asked. "I have to get this poncho on."

Fen tucked the hose back into the wheelbarrow while I put the orange rain poncho on and looked down at myself.

"I look like a total McDoofus, but it does cover the hose surprisingly well," I said. "Let's boogie!"

Fen pushed the wheelbarrow down the sidewalk and I walked alongside him. The town of

Nevermind isn't very big—only a few hundred houses tucked into small streets, a charming little downtown with an ice cream shack and a burger hut, and a lot of secrets. I hoped the coordinates Vexler had sent over would lead us somewhere close by. Which reminded me of something important.

"We don't know where we're going," I said. "Barker hasn't texted us the address yet."

"Oh yeah," Fen said. He stopped pushing the wheelbarrow. Unfortunately, at that moment, Naddy Burns appeared on her bicycle. The downside of living in a town as small as Nevermind is the good chance that you'll see people like Naddy Burns more than once in the same day.

She rolled up and skidded to a stop.

"What's up, traffic cone?" Naddy said. I had to give her credit; I did look like a traffic cone in my orange poncho. After she stopped laughing, she kept talking. "You've been burned! Because you look like a traffic cone."

"Yeah, I got it," I groaned. "What can we do for you, Naddy?"

"What's in the wheelbarrow?" she asked. "All your failures?" For a few seconds, she laughed hysterically, but then she was all business. "No seriously. What's in the wheelbarrow?"

"None of your business," Fen said.

"Zip it, yard gnome," Naddy said, and she turned back to me and stared.

She got off her bike and flicked the kickstand, then walked right up to the wheelbarrow and tried to move the tarp out of the way.

"I wouldn't do that if I were you," Fen said.

"Oh reeeeally?" Naddy said in her snarkiest voice.

She bent down for a closer look and came face-to-face with a furry hose at full vacuum power. Unfortunately, Naddy didn't move fast enough, and the hose stuck to her forehead.

The Snerb was trying to eat Naddy Burns. She got both hands around the hose and tried to pull it off, but this thing was stuck like a nuclear magnet. Naturally, Naddy started screaming. Now I felt bad for her. Plus, it was turning into a spectacle that was sure to draw the attention of half the neighborhood. She fell over and started rolling around on someone's front yard, pulling on the hose as hard as she could.

I had to do something. *Think fast, Jenny!*

On instinct, I grabbed the fuzzy orange hose stuck to my armpit and yanked it as hard as I could. This seemed to distract the Snerb just long enough to lower the sucking power on the hose, and Naddy Burns broke free. The hose flopped around like a snake, then recoiled under the tarp.

When Naddy Burns sat up, she had a giant red circle on her forehead. On the plus side, she was speechless for once in her life, and that gave me just enough time to explain what was going on. And by that, I mean I made up a story.

"So sorry, Naddy," I said. "We tried to warn

you. Fen and I started our own business. We run a car vacuuming service and we're going around offering our latest special. So, yeah . . . that's what's under the tarp. A giant vacuum cleaner. I have no idea how that thing got turned on."

Naddy stood up and wobbled back and forth a couple of times. "What is wrong with you two?!"

"You've got some yard in your hair," Fen said.

Naddy Burns looked at the wheelbarrow and sidestepped nervously toward her bike. She didn't even bother glaring at us. She just rode away without another word. I got the feeling she wasn't going to be bothering us anymore—at least not today.

"That actually went better than I would have expected," Fen said.

"I think you might be right," I agreed.

"Burns got burned," Fen agreed.

That was actually sort of funny. I laughed. Then he laughed. Before we knew it, we were both cracking up hysterically—so much so that the Snerb hoses came out and joined the fun, twirling in the air right along with us. Unfortunately, that's when things took a turn for the worse.

One of the hoses locked onto a mailbox and pulled it right out of the sidewalk.

"It ate the mail!" Fen yelled.

The hoses were getting bigger before our very eyes, and they were also getting longer. One of them attached itself to the exhaust pipe of a pickup truck sitting in a driveway, another one was guzzling dirty water out of a bird bath.

"Um, Jenster?" Fen said. "We have a problem."

I spun toward the wheelbarrow and my jaw dropped.

The tarp was expanding.

Have you ever had one of those popcorn containers with the foil top? You know, the ones that expand as the popcorn pops until it's like an alien head sitting on your stovetop? That's what was happening to the tarp covering the wheelbarrow.

The Snerb was also starting to leak out the sides of the tarp, orange fuzzy layers of goop reaching for the sidewalk.

"The bungee cords aren't going to hold for much longer," Fen said.

My phone dinged and I pulled it out.

"Barker sent the address!"

"Where to?!" Fen asked as he tried to pick up the wheelbarrow by the handles. Before I could answer, he grunted, "You're going to have to take one side—it's getting too heavy!"

In case you were wondering, if he'd given me a chance, I would have said: *Alleyway in the Old Park.* Point is, I knew exactly where we were going, and it was only two blocks away. But could we make it there before the wheelbarrow blew its top?

"Grab your side," I yelled, then I pulled on the orange fuzzy hose attached to my armpit as hard as I could, and all the arms extending out of the Snerb recoiled into the darkness under the tarp.

At least the terror that came from my armpit was still obeying me, but how much longer would that last? With each new command I felt less certain the Snerb would listen to me.

We each took one of the handles and lifted the wheelbarrow onto its wheel.

Then we looked at each other and yelled the same word.

"RUN!"

CHAPTER 13

TERROR ON OLD PARK ROAD

We took a left at the first corner, nearly tipping the wheelbarrow over when we hit a pothole and approached the final turn.

"Why does it keep getting bigger?!" Fen screamed.

"I have no idea!" I yelled back. "Hard right turn!"

We swung wide onto a dirt road and the towering wheelbarrow full of Snerb teetered one way and then the other, hose arms and globs of orange fur flopping out from under the tarp. Soon, trees and dense underbrush lined both sides of the road and an endless canopy of leaves blotted out the sun overhead.

"It's a dead end," Fen gasped. "Are you sure this is the right place?"

"I'm positive. Barker's directions were very clear: *Alleyway in the Old Park.*"

The Old Park, also known as Cotton Candy Land by some, was one of the places in Nevermind nobody went after dark, not even the adults. (There was also the abandoned mall with its rumors of zombies, the house on Ham Hill, and about a dozen other spots in Nevermind I don't have time to explain. But the Old Park was *for sure* on the list of places not to go after dark.) It was split in two by the narrow dirt road we were on, and both sides of the Old Park were haunted. It's a long story for another time, but since we're friends, I'll give you the short version in three quick points while we wait for Vexler to show up:

1. The property on one side of the Old Park Road was once owned by Terrance Flem, a reclusive blowhard who hated three things: loud noises, kids, and kids. He couldn't stand kids so much he always mentioned them twice. *I can't stand kids. And I can't stand kids!*

2. The property on the other side of the Old Park Road was owned by Fletcher Dingman, a Walt Disney wannabe who opened a theme park on the property with rundown fair rides and cotton candy. He called it Cotton Candy Land and it went bankrupt nine days after it opened.

3. It is universally agreed in Nevermind that Terrance Flem, who could not stand kids, drove a forklift into all the rides at the stroke of midnight on the eighth

day Cotton Candy Land was open. This began a feud that lasted twenty-four hours, culminating in the disappearance of both men. No one knows where either of them went. It is widely agreed on by every kid in Nevermind that Flem and Dingman went to war and neither of them survived. They haunt the Old Park to this day.

The only other thing I'll mention about the Old Park is the rides are still there, rusted and ruined, some of them tipped over and grown over with ivy. I'll take you there someday when I'm a little less busy, but for now . . .

A big, loud truck was barreling down the dirt road I was standing on! I wouldn't call it a monster truck, but it was close. Giant knobby tires carried it across the road and the bed of the truck had high walls made of steel.

"Wow, that thing is really moving," Fen said. "Should we jump into the woods?"

"No way! The ghosts of Flem and Dingman are in there!"

"Who's Flem Flingman?!" Fen yelled.

I'd forgotten Fen was new in town and had no idea we were standing on ghostly ground, but it didn't matter because the pickup truck hit the breaks, fishtailed back and forth, and came to a stop four feet in front of our wheelbarrow. A fantastic plume of dust filled the air and knocked our line of sight down to about two feet.

As the dust started to clear, something else came barreling toward us out of the haze. It was moving fast, swirls of airborne debris curling around handlebars and someone on a bike. The bike turned hard into a skid and showered me and Fen with gravel and dirt clods.

Barker Mifflin had arrived on the scene.

"What's under the tarp?" Barker asked. He was all business.

It was no time to worry about what Barker Mifflin might think.

"Something terrible grew out of my armpit," I said. "It's under the tarp. And it's still attached to my armpit."

I peeled the orange poncho off and held up my arm. The tube running from me to the wheelbarrow looked like an orange garden hose piled up at my feet.

One of the Snerb hoses flopped around in the air like a cooked noodle and headed toward Barker. It was on a collision course with his face, but faster than a lightning bolt, Barker pulled a pancake spatula out of his backpack. He slapped the hose one way and then the other, and the Snerb made a loud rumbling sound under the tarp.

"It's growing again!" I yelled.

The tarp started to rip down the middle and the hideous eyeball broke into the open air. It glanced at me, then Fen, and finally Barker. The eyeball locked eyes on the pancake spatula, and then all twelve hoses were pointed in one direction, sucking up dust as they bore down on Barker Mifflin.

"Run, Barker!" Fen yelled.

The spatula flew through the air and *flump*, into a hose it went. Barker hit the peddles on his bike and tried to ride away, but the sucking power of so many vacuum hoses was too powerful. Leaves and rocks and tree limbs swirled in the air and disappeared into the Snerb, but the giant eyeball kept staring at Barker.

"Get off the bike!" I screamed through the storm of debris.

Barker jumped off the bike and barrel-rolled down the dirt road. The bike flew up into the air and landed thirty feet up in a tree in the Old Park.

"Fen, get to the truck!" I screamed. "We need help!"

"I'll distract this thing!" Barker yelled. "You make a run for it!"

Barker stood up and started waving his arms around. "Hey, cyclops face! Over here!"

The giant eyeball darted around, searching for the voice, and landed on Barker.

"That's it, come on!" Barker yelled.

He put his hands behind his shoulders like he was about to pull out two samurai swords, and for a second, I thought we might have a chance. But then Barker's hands flew forward and each one held a fly swatter.

"You have *got* to get better weapons!" I yelled.

Fen took off running as the eyeball tore farther through the tarp and one of the bungee cords snapped in two. We had a minute, maybe two, and the Snerb was going to break free. What would happen then? Would it drag me into the Old Park and eat me for lunch? Would it spin me around from my armpit like a lasso at a rodeo?

The pickup truck revved its engine and a

loudspeaker attached to the hood crackled to life. A woman's voice with a German accent filled the Old Park.

"Extraction process has begun. Please proceed to the truck. I repeat, proceed to the truck."

The passenger door flew open and Fen dove in headfirst.

"Get to the truck, Barker!" I screamed.

Another bungee cord snapped in two and the tarp ripped even more. The wheelbarrow wobbled and shook like it was about to explode.

"I can't leave you behind!" Barker yelled as he slapped orange hoses with flyswatters. I had to admit, the flyswatters were working better then I'd expected.

"Just go! I'm right behind you!"

But I knew the truth. Where was I going to go? I couldn't get away from the terror that came from my armpit. I was attached to it.

Barker ran for the pickup and jumped in. The passenger door slammed behind him, and that's when I realized something weird from where I was standing in the middle of the road.

There was nobody in the driver's seat. It was just my two friends, no one else.

The engine revved and the back tires started spinning. Vexler's voice boomed through the loudspeaker again.

"Beginning stage two."

Where was she?! And what was stage two?

The truck barreled down the road, dirt flying and the giant wheels bouncing over rocks and tree limbs.

"Wait, what's happening?" I asked out loud as I stood there like a lump on a log.

I saw Barker and Fen white-knuckling the dashboard, mouths and eyes wide open, screaming as the truck slammed into the wheelbarrow.

I felt something tug at my armpit.

And then I was flying through the air.

CHAPTER 14

ELEVEN SECONDS

Everything I'm about to explain happened in eleven seconds. Lucky for you, it felt like it was in slow motion, so I remember every last detail. And since you're one of my all-time best friends, I'll tell you the whole story in eleven one-second bullet points! Because you know how much I love lists. Here we go!

The amazing list of eleven things that happened in eleven seconds:

THE FIRST SECOND: I saw a very large truck barreling toward the wheelbarrow. My two friends, Barker and Fen, were in that truck. They looked like they were screaming, but I couldn't hear them because the truck was *super* loud. They were both staring at me.

THE SECOND SECOND: Right before the truck hit the wheelbarrow, I looked at the giant Snerb eyeball. It was wide open, staring at the truck. This seemed like a good time to jump out of the way, so I took two quick steps and dove for the side of the road.

THE THIRD SECOND: The truck hit the wheelbarrow. The sound this made was like a symphony warming up, but the instruments were buckets of fart putty, wet mops slapping a gym floor, buckets of water being dumped on a driveway, mashed potatoes hitting a plastic lunch tray, toilets flushing, and pulling a bunch of boots out of a swimming pool full of cooked oatmeal. This is the sound of a very large Snerb exploding out of a wheelbarrow. You're welcome.

THE FOURTH SECOND: The Snerb went airborne. It looked like a jellyfish smooshing and squishing and expanding and stretching into the sky. All the many air hoses flopped around like ramen noodles and the whole thing was strangely beautiful, like a sunset. Okay maybe not a sunset, but still pretty, in a weird way.

THE FIFTH SECOND: The furry tube—or hose or whatever it was that connected my armpit to this thing flying through the air—started to pull. It was stretchier than I expected, like the biggest rubber band in the history of rubber bands.

Naturally, I raised my hand like I wanted to answer a question in class, because a very powerful rubber band was pulling my armpit toward the sun.

THE SIXTH SECOND: I flew into the air. For the entire length of the sixth second, I thought this was incredibly cool. I am Jenny Kim, the girl who could fly.

THE SEVENTH SECOND: I realized I wasn't a bird or a plane or a UFO and flying was not in my skill set. I was not supposed to be flying. I went through the eight stages of fear while flying through the air attached to a Snerb: crying, screaming, punching the air, kicking the air, summersaults in the air, pretending to swim the backstroke, Yoga poses, and looking down. Looking down caused me to scream again.

THE EIGHTH SECOND: As I was screaming and staring at the ground, I realized two things:

1. I was really far from the ground.
2. The truck was doing a burn out at the end of the dirt road. It was turning around and coming back.

THE NINTH SECOND: The Snerb reached the end of its rise into the sky and began falling back to Earth. The big eyeball saw me as it went by and seemed to feel sorry for me, which I appreciated. I waved.

THE TENTH SECOND: The hose attached to my armpit tightened again and pulled me toward the ground right behind the Snerb. It appeared we were both headed for trouble.

THE ELEVENTH SECOND: The truck skidded to a stop. Dust billowed in a giant circle underneath me, and the Snerb landed in the truck bed. This caused the Snerb to spread out like a water balloon squishing onto the pavement before it explodes, very useful for someone in my situation because the truck bed, with its high metal walls, had basically turned into a swimming pool. Half a second later, I landed on the Snerb for the second time in a half hour.

Pretty amazing, right? I mean the fact that I even survived is a big pile of marshmallow miracle sauce. It's amazing! I laid on top of the Snerb like a snow angel and laughed. But then the loudspeaker on the front of the truck crackled to life again.

"Please exit the truck bed and find your way to the door," Vexler said. "Initiating stage three."

I heard the sound of the truck door opening

somewhere down below. The Snerb had survived the fall and it was starting to make some new sounds I hadn't heard before.

"Exit truck bed immediately," Vexler said in her calm German accent. "Snerb is entering phase nine. Exposure no longer safe. I repeat, exit truck bed immediately."

I sat up and felt the Snerb I was sitting on with my hands. It was furry, like a green on a golf course.

"Hey, what's this thing?" I asked out loud.

I reached out and touched something about the size of a blender. It was white.

"There's another," I said, because a second one had popped out right next to me. "What are these things?"

They were appearing all around me, emerging from the depth of the Snerb, like objects floating up out of the ocean.

"Wait just a second here," I said.

I figured out what they were as they continued

to pop out in a circle all around me, because I was also sinking.

The Snerb was growing teeth.

And I was sitting in what was about to become its mouth.

CHAPTER 15

THE DUNGEONS OF SNERBVILLE

The spot I was sitting in very quickly became a hole. I fell right into it, with rows of sharp teeth all around me. Picture a whirlpool of slime, pulling me down into a sea of Snerb.

"HEEEEEELP!" I screamed.

The loudspeaker sputtered back to life, and Vexler's voice returned. It was maddeningly calm.

"Sending mechanical claw. Hold, please."

All I could do at that point was hang onto a giant slimy tooth and hope the mouth I was dangling inside of wouldn't slam shut. Something tightened around my feet and my hands started to slide down a slippery Snerb tooth. Gurgling, burping, slimy sounds roared all around me, but I could hear something mechanical happening over my head. I looked up and a metal claw was lowering toward me.

"You gotta be kidding me," I said.

The metal claw opened its jaws, lowered into the mouth of the Snerb, and clamped around my waist.

"Not so tight!" I screamed, because the claw felt like a belt notched four sizes too small.

"Begin extraction," Vexler said over the loud-speaker.

I felt like a cork stuck in a bottle as the claw lifted me and the Snerb tightened its grip around my feet. When I was halfway out of the mouth the teeth started to close more quickly.

"Pull harder!" I shouted.

There was a loud *pop* sound as my feet came

free and I pulled my feet up to my chest just in time for the mouth to slam shut.

"Extraction complete," Vexler said. "Please use passenger window to enter vehicle."

The claw was attached to the roof of the truck and it swung me to the passenger side, where the window rolled down. This actually made sense to me even if it wasn't going to be easy climbing through the window. I couldn't go through the door because it would close onto the hose stuck to my armpit, and that was sure to send the Snerb into a rage.

"You're okay?!" Fen said, slack-jawed. He sounded more surprised than relieved. Not that I could blame him. I was hanging from a giant mechanical claw like a slime-covered bag of potatoes.

Without warning, the claw opened and dropped me on the dirt road, but I was only three feet of the ground, so I survived. "Proceeding to destination," Vexler said.

"Get in here," Barker commanded from inside the truck. The engine revved and the wheels started spinning.

In a flash, I dove for the door and grabbed the edge of the open window just as the truck took off like a funny car on a drag racing strip. This time I was too scared to scream. My legs flopped around like the Snerb's tentacles while Fen and Barker grabbed my arms and tried to haul me inside.

"Hang on, Jen-Jen," Fen grunted,. "We got you!"

There was a huge BANG from inside the truck bed and we swerved hard to the left and nearly hit a tree. Another BANG and we swerved to the right, went up on two wheels, and some- how managed to make the turn onto the main road.

"The Snerb is trying to escape," Barker yelled. He was maddeningly calm.

Fen and Barker pulled on my arms at the

same time and I tumbled into the truck, landing in a heap on the floor.

"All parties accounted for," Vexler said. "Arrival in six minutes."

"Where are we going?" I asked, climbing up into the seat between Barker and Fen.

"Don't look at me," Barker said. "I barely know what's going on."

Fen squinted out the window. "Vexler can see us, wherever she is. So she must be able to hear us too. She's in control."

I wondered if he'd finally gone insane, but then I realized he was right. After all, we were in a speeding van with nobody at the wheel. Vexler was controlling the truck from somewhere, and she was the only person who might have any idea what was going on. It was time for her to answer my one all-important question.

"Vexler!" I yelled over the roar of the truck engine. "Tell me what's growing out of my armpit!"

So she did. And since you're my new bestie,

I'll spare you her three-minute answer, because
Vexler can make even the worst disaster sound
like a total yawn-fest. Let's just say, my mind
was blown. Some details I already knew, some I
didn't, but hearing it from the scientist herself
made me queasy. It didn't help that we were in
a driverless truck, careening around sharp cor-
ners, speeding toward whatever lay in store for
us. I learned three basic facts:

FACT NUMBER ONE: Colossal Chemistry
made hundreds of Snerbs and they're
all still alive.

FACT NUMBER TWO: Snerbs were created
to eat garbage and pollution. The more
garbage and air pollution they eat, the
bigger they get and the faster they grow.

FACT NUMBER THREE: Colossal Chemistry
dug a massive system of underground

tunnels to hold all the failed Snerb experiments. Vexler is quite sure there are at least a hundred Snerbs in the underground tunnels. The system of tunnels is called the Dungeons of Snerbville.

"You can't be serious," I said when she was finished. "*Snerbville?!* That sounds like a happy place where kids go on rides and eat candy."

"I have to agree with you there, Jenster," Fen said. "You'd think a bunch of scientists could come up with a better name. Like . . . Smash Town! No wait—the Dungeon of Danger!"

Barker Mifflin was clearly fascinated by Vexler's information. I could see by the look on his face, glazed over and half smiling, that he wasn't as scared as he was fascinated by everything Vexler had said. He was imagining himself in go-time survival mode deep in the Dungeons of Snerbville. He'd been waiting for something like this his entire life. Neat for him, but I only had one thing on my mind.

"How do I get this thing off my armpit?!" I demanded.

There was no answer, just a crackling sound from the speaker, followed by dead air. A moment later, Vexler was back, though sounding more sheepish than she had before.

"I'm sorry to say, if you touch a Snerb it will make you a host. You can remove the Snerb during the first two hours, when it's small, although it is quite painful. Beyond the two-hour mark lies only danger and destruction."

I opened my mouth, but I wasn't sure what I wanted to ask.

"I think Jen-Jen needs you to be more specific," Fen said into the silence. "What kind of danger and destruction?"

"The Snerb will always eat the host in the end." She said.

Static filled the loudspeaker.

"Hey!" I barked. "You made this thing! You can't just let it eat people!"

We took a sharp turn and all leaned hard to the right. Fen got the worst of it, squished into the door.

The static cleared. "There is *one* way to safely remove a mature Snerb from an armpit," Vexler said after a long silence. "But it has to be done at the right time, in the right way."

Before she could get to exactly *how* to stop hosting the terror that grew out of my armpit, a gigantic noise came from the back of the truck. It sounded like a semitruck driving over a washing machine.

"What was that?" Barker said. For some reason, he now had a flyswatter in each hand, as if that could protect him. He was always "commando-ready if things went pear-shaped." His words.

Fen leaned out the window and stared back at the Snerb. He looked a little greenish when he ducked back inside.

"We might have a small problem," he said.

The truck shook with a sickening jolt. We rocked one way and then the other, swerved onto someone's lawn, and clobbered a mailbox on our way back to the street.

"Give us the intel, Fen," Barker said. "What's happening back there?"

Fen Stenson finally spilled the beans, and it seemed to me that we should have expected it all along.

"The Snerb is eating the truck."

CHAPTER 16

SNERB-O-MATIC!

The Snerb made quick business of two metal walls and the tailgate, then it went after the back tires.

"Arriving at destination," Vexler said in her calm German accent. "Prepare for impact."

The Snerb chomped down on one of the back wheels and tore it right off the truck.

"Prepare for impact?" I repeated.

That's when I saw that we were back at Colossal Chemistry. We crashed through the heavy metal gate at the same moment the Snerb ate wheel number two. We were suddenly pitched upward, staring at the sky. Sparks flew as we dragged the back end of the truck on the axels. I peered over the dashboard to see that we were fishtailing down a ramp, toward a garage door. It was opening, but slowly. Too slowly . . .

I squeezed my eyes shut.

"We made it!" Fen yelled.

Vexler had timed it perfectly. You gotta love those scientists, am I right? We slipped underneath, with about an inch to spare. But my joy was short-lived. We slid into a 360, spinning around and around until finally coming to a stop in a shower of sparks and burned rubber. The garage door closed behind us. We were trapped.

"Exit vehicle in five, four—"

It was Vexler, counting us down. But why was she counting down to exit the truck?

"Whoa," Barker said.

I followed his gaze through the back window of the truck.

Vexler kept counting us down!

"—three, two, one—"

The giant eyeball was staring at us, but it wasn't as big as a frying pan anymore.

It was about the size of a dishwasher.

It was then, while we stared out the window, that the eyeball reared up into the air and the open mouth of the Snerb appeared. It was like looking into a dark, dreary, wet cavern full of jagged rocks and dripping slime.

If not for Vexler's voice, I would have been paralyzed long past when I could have escaped.

"GO, GO, GO!"

Fen threw open the passenger door and all three of us tumbled out on top of each other in a pile of screaming terror. In a flash we were up and sprinting away from the horrible grinding sound behind us. By the time I turned around, the truck was completely gone. All that remained was a big, empty warehouse. And one giant Snerb.

"How could *that* thing have come from my *armpit*?" I asked out loud.

A furry hose extended from me, across the floor. And there, in all its hideous orange glory, sat the terror that came from my armpit. The hoses had gotten longer and wider, dancing slowly in the air like vipers waiting to strike. Basketball-sized holes sucked air in and out of the body, and the gargantuan mouth hung open. The grill of the truck was stuck to one of the teeth.

The eye stared down at us, huge and bloodshot, wild with hunger for more, more, more. And there was only one thing left for it to eat.

Us.

The Snerb sloshed forward until it was towering over us and then the mouth opened.

It was then that I remembered there was a time, not long ago, when the Snerb had listened to me. It had trusted me. And I'd had about all I was going to take from the thing I was attached to.

"Don't. You. Dare!" I yelled up at the eyeball.

The Snerb reared back and the eye softened. It looked surprised, like it wasn't exactly sure what to do next.

"I carried you out of Colossal Chemistry!" I yelled. "I protected you! I took care of you! And in case you haven't been paying attention, I'm attached to you!"

I held up the floppy rope or hose or whatever it was that started in my armpit, stretched across the floor, and ended in a giant blob of orange fuzz that was bigger than a bus.

"I mean let's be honest," Fen whispered. "We've been trying to get rid of this thing since it showed up."

"Back me up here. I'm trying to stop it from eating us."

"Oh, right, sorry," Fen whispered, then he yelled up into the air. "You can't just go around eating kids! It's undignified!"

The Snerb leaned a little closer.

"Listen," I said as nicely as I could, "I know

you're trying to eat garbage and pollution. I get that you have a noble purpose. You clean up the world! That's really great. But we're not garbage. We're people."

The Snerb seemed to understand what I was saying, or at least understand enough that it was having to think twice. I finally realized something I hadn't before. The Snerb was reacting to how I felt. If I was screaming in terror, the Snerb went bananas. If I was calm, it was calm. I was feeling pretty good about myself, but then there came a big noise from directly behind us. I whirled around to see what it was.

A giant round door, taller than a telephone pole, was opening.

It was the first time I ever set eyes on the real Dr. Vexler. She looked just like she did in her picture, only she wasn't wearing the lab coat. She was dressed more like an explorer, every- thing tan colored with lots of pockets. She wore a Panama hat.

"You're going to need a Snerb-O-Matic," she said. "It's the only way."

"A Snerb-O-Matic?" I repeated.

"Jenny, I'm going to need you to stay calm," she said. "That thing is going to respond to how you're doing. If you become too nervous, it might crash through the garage door and eat every garbage can in town."

"So no pressure then," I said.

"Very little," she said. "All you have to do is stand there."

She looked at Fen and Barker. "You two, get over here."

Of course, the two boys had to huddle up and talk shop.

"Are we doing this?" Fen asked.

"Not sure we have a lot of options," Barker answered. "And she seems to know what she's doing."

"We could run," Fen said.

"I say we go see what she wants," Barker said.

"I've got two cans of corn if we need them and I'm a good shot. I also have a wooden spoon."

"You have weird weapons," Fen said.

"Thanks."

Vexler was tapping her foot on the concrete floor, nervous or impatient or both.

"The longer you two stand there, the more likely you'll be on the dinner menu," Vexler said. "How about we get the show on the road?"

Fen and Barker nodded at each other and walked slowly toward Vexler, who looked small standing in the maw of the door. The Snerb made curious glugging sounds, as if it, too, wondered what Vexler wanted and what lay beyond the giant opening she had come through.

"Steady now," I said. "We're just standing around, nothing to worry about. Or I guess you're not standing since you don't have legs. But you do have those fancy vacuum noodle hoses. I think I'll call them Hose-O-Matics. Good for you."

I know, I know—I need better small talk.

I bit my lip, trying to listen for the others, but I couldn't really hear what was going on. I only caught bits and pieces of what they were saying.

". . . ike a backpack."

"Just hold down the trigger . . ."

"This way."

A moment later, Barker returned. He was alone, holding what looked like an industrial leaf blower. He also had what looked like an orange jetpack strapped to his back. A hose ran out of the bottom and into the darkness behind the door.

"Let me guess," I said. "That's a Snerb-O-Matic?"

"You know it," Barker said, "I'm gonna need you to start the engine."

"The engine?"

"It's like a lawnmower. Just pull on the cord."

I found the handle and pulled the cord, but the engine only sputtered.

"Give it another go," Barker said.

I pulled two more times and then some sort of gas engine fired up and idled like a chainsaw.

Barker revved the engine, giving it a test, and smoggy air bubbled out of the leaf blower.

"I'm goin' in!" Barker yelled, and he took off running toward the Snerb.

"You got this, Barker!" Fen yelled from somewhere far behind me.

"This day just keeps getting weirder," I said.

Barker ran right up to the Snerb and pointed the Snerb-O-Matic up toward all the flopping hoses. Then he held down the trigger on the Snerb-O-Matic and gray smog poured into the room.

"Feeding time for Snerbo!" Barker said.

"Come and get it!" Fen yelled.

It turns out spewing pollution in front of a Snerb has basically the same effect as putting a bucket of slop in front of a piglet. The furry hoses sucked up smog as fast as Barker could dish it out.

"Slowly now," Vexler yelled from behind me. "One step at a time. Move toward the door."

Barker started walking backward toward the giant round door. Everything was going to plan, or so it seemed, until the Snerb-O-Matic sputtered and coughed and died.

"I need a restart!" Barker yelled.

"Coming!"

I was standing between Barker and Vexler, only a few steps away, but the vacuum sucking power of the hoses was completely out of control. They'd gotten a taste of pure pollution, and it had sent the Snerb into hyperdrive. It was like standing in the path of a massive wind turbine, dragging us closer and closer on the slick concrete floor.

"Come on, Jenny!" Barker screamed through the whirl of wind. "Here comes its mouth!"

The gaping hole surrounded by teeth was descending toward Barker Mifflin, and I fumbled for the starter handle. It wobbled out of my hand. I reached again and gripped it as tightly as I could. Three pulls later and all I'd gotten was a few sputters.

"It's not working!" I yelled.

"There's a green button on the side," Vexler said in her maddeningly calm voice. I could barely hear what she was saying over the ruckus. "Push it three times and try again."

I searched the side of the engine and found the button.

"One, two, three," I said as I pushed it three times.

"We're out of time, Jenny!" Barker yelled. He was like a wall in front of me, blocking the brunt of the hoses, but it didn't matter.

The mouth of the Snerb had landed on the floor with Barker and me inside. It was dark in there, but I could still see the teeth as they scraped across the floor.

I grabbed the starter handle again and pulled the cord as hard as I could!

I heard a snap.

THE TERROR IN JENNY'S ARMPIT

"Oh no," I said.

Unfortunately, I'd pulled the cord right out of the engine. The end of the rope dangled at my feet as one of the teeth touched my shoe. But the engine made a series of sounds—*glug glug pop bing pow—ROooOOaaaAARRR!*

The engine was going again!

"Here comes dessert, Snerbo!" Barker yelled as he blasted gobs of thick smog straight up into the mouth of the beast.

The Snerb's mouth opened wide and lolled upward, drinking in gobs of toxic waste.

"It might be best if you run," Vexler advised through the bullhorn.

The Snerb-O-Matic started sputtering, delivering less fog garbage than it had before, but Barker had reached the enormous round door. Then I lost sight of him. Actually, I lost sight of everyone. Fen Stenson, Barker Mifflin, Dr. Vexler—they all vanished. The last to go was the Snerb, through the gargantuan door, following what little smog there was left to eat.

The round door rolled nearly closed. There was only a small gap left where soft light spilled out onto the warehouse floor. I was all alone, but I wasn't free.

The Snerb was still attached to my armpit.

And the Snerb was pulling.

CHAPTER 17

IS THAT A BLOWTORCH?!

A vast thundering sound came from behind the round door, echoing across the empty space of the warehouse. The terror that came from my armpit didn't sound happy. Was it because it was now trapped in the Dungeons of Snerbville? Or was it because I wasn't there with it?

"Hey! Is anyone there?!" I pleaded. "Hello?"

The Snerb kept pulling me slowly forward, one step at a time, and the space between me and the door was getting dangerously short.

Vexler's voice boomed into the warehouse

through speakers high up on the warehouse walls.

"Hold, please," she said.

Wild sounds of a struggle behind the giant round door echoed into the warehouse. The hose attached to my armpit slackened so I ran as far as I could into the warehouse. But then there was a groan and something that sounded like a wet sneeze from far away and the hose jerked harder than it ever had before. It pulled me off my feet.

The Snerb was dragging me across the floor!

Barker Mifflin darted through the small gap followed by Fen. I tried to stand up but couldn't and tumbled forward as the orange furry hose kept pulling.

"I'm in trouble here guys!" I yelled.

Vexler's voice filled the warehouse, and for the first time, she was yelling: "NOW, FEN STENSON, NOW!"

Fen was holding something that had a flame coming out of one end.

"Is that a blowtorch?!" I asked.

The flame grew longer and bluer and more dangerous looking.

"NO WAY you're using that on my armpit!" I yelled.

"Closing security door in ten seconds," Vexler said. "Any longer and we'll risk a full-blown Snerb infestation."

"She's right, Jenny," Barker said. "There are a lot of Snerbs behind that door. We gotta cut you loose."

"But a *blowtorch*?! There must be a better way!"

"Ten, nine, eight . . ." Vexler's countdown started, and the round door began to close. The gap was only big enough to keep from crushing the hose.

"What if we let the door close on the hose?" I argued. "That could totally work! I'll just wander around Nevermind with a furry orange rope hanging from my armpit for the rest of my life. I can do that."

I was only a few feet from the door now, and the distant sound of the angry Snerb felt farther away than it ever had before.

"You can't live like that," Fen said.

"Five, four, three . . ."

"Trust me, Jen-Jen," Fen said.

The Snerb pulled one more time, harder than before, and I was flush against the door. The only thing left of the Snerb that wasn't on the other side was me.

"Two . . ."

There was nothing left to do but trust my friends, so I nodded, closed my eyes, and held my arm up.

"One . . ."

I heard the blowtorch hiss and whine, and when the flame landed in my armpit, it sounded like a saw cutting through iron. I opened my eyes and saw sparks flying everywhere.

"Hold still; we got this!" Fen screamed.

"Door closing," Vexler said.

One more burst of sparks and then I heard a loud *snap* sound. The end of the Snerb slithered and shook and flopped. It disappeared into the gap and the door slammed shut.

"Extraction complete," Vexler's voice announced, as calm as ever.

"We did it!" Fen yelled. "We totally did it!"

"We sure did," Barker agreed.

I stood up and lifted my arm over my head. I pulled my T-shirt back so I could see my armpit. About three inches of orange hose hung there.

"You missed a spot," I said.

"It's not a blowtorch," Fen explained as the end of the hose shriveled and started to turn to orange dust.

"It's a molecule-busting laser torch," Fen said.

The tube shriveled more and more and then turned entirely to dust. I felt my armpit, smooth and completely normal.

"It's gone," I whispered. "It's actually gone."

"It sure is!" Fen said. "Plus, we have this cool laser torch!"

"Give me that thing before you hurt yourself," Barker said.

I had to agree, a weapon like that was safer in Barker Mifflin's hands than any other kid I knew.

I heard the garage door opening at the other end of the warehouse.

"Please exit the building," Vexler said over the speakers. "And tell no one what you've seen. Dangerous people are watching! Leave and don't come back!"

We began walking toward the garage door and a part of me wished we could tell everyone what had happened. What a story! But then I thought about the punchline—Jenny had a monster living in her armpit—and I was glad Vexler told us to keep it quiet.

"You guys wanna come over for dinner?" I asked.

"I'd love to!" Fen said.

"I've got hand-to-hand combat training in half an hour," Barker said. "Maybe next time."

The garage door started going down again and we ran for the exit. Vexler knew how to keep people on a schedule.

"What's it like in there?" I asked.

"Where?" Fen replied.

"In Snerbville."

Fen and I both turned to Barker, who had a faraway look in his eye.

"There's a whole world under there," he mused. "Tunnels and chambers, bridges and lagoons and secret passageways. I'm going there someday; just you wait."

Fen flashed an awkward smile. "Uh . . . that's great."

"Barker Mifflin, you were made for that place," I said.

"Don't you know it," he agreed.

Fen and I went one way, Barker went the other, and we strolled toward my house in the twilight of a quiet evening in Nevermind. I know this might sound hard to believe, but if something like this was going to happen, it was bound to happen in Nevermind. It's not even the strangest thing that's ever happened here. And hey, I got a new best friend, I grew a creature out of my armpit who now lives happily in someplace called Snerbville, and I only have a few lingering questions.

Who is Vexler, really?

Where exactly is Snerbville and what's down there?

And will Barker Mifflin ever go back there?

I'm glad you were along for the ride, but you know what we say in the town of Nevermind, right? We say . . . *never mind*. In other words, pretend this didn't happen, tell no one, and don't try to find Nevermind on a map, because if you think a monster growing out of my armpit is weird, wait until you hear about the forty-foot chicken terrorizing a farm just north of town.

But that's a story for another time.

EPILOGUE

NINE DAYS LATER

Doctor Vexler was sitting in the control room monitoring the Dungeons of Snerbville while drinking a cup of tea that had gone cold. She had eaten a can of peaches and a cracker for dinner and, as usual, it had been uninspiring.

It seemed she was destined to endure another night on the watch, a duty she carried like a heavy suitcase on a trip to nowhere. From far away, she heard a hose sucking goop from a pipe with a sickening slurp. She had grown used to these kinds of sounds in the miles and miles of underground tunnels and chambers, but there was one sound she hadn't heard in quite some time.

She heard it now, a piercing blare ripping through the control room, repeating like a siren. She tapped some blue keys on a strange, glowing keyboard, and the sound stopped. A voice appeared, distant and full of static.

"Station three to control room! Station three to control room! Do you read me?"

Vexler hadn't heard from station three in over a month, and she worried the events of nine days ago with Jenny Kim and her two nitwit friends had been discovered. Had someone seen them?

It suddenly felt like half the dry cracker was lodged in her throat, so she coughed and gulped down the last of the cold tea.

"Station three to control room!"

Vexler reached across the blue keyboard and warily held down a red button with the number three on it.

"Vexler here," she said. "Are you on a secure line?"

"There's no time for that! It's me, McFadden!"

"What seems to be the problem?" Vexler asked while thinking to herself: *not this bozo again.*

"Open Tunnel 21 immediately!"

This was bad news. The opening for Tunnel 21 was large, the biggest of all the entry points.

"I'll need an authorization code," Vexler said in her calm German accent. She was nothing if not cool under pressure.

"There's no time for codes!" McFadden screamed. "Open Tunnel 21!"

This was how they'd gotten into so much trouble to begin with, by not following any of the rules. For all she knew, McFadden only wanted to dump a truck full of garbage into Tunnel 21, an unauthorized act of award-winning stupidity.

Unfortunately for Vexler, McFadden was technically her boss. He held most of the cards.

It was he and the other blockhead who would decide when she would complete her time in the Dungeons of Snerbville. She calculated the risk, tapped out a few commands, and let her finger hover over a pink key shaped like a diamond.

"Opening Tunnel 21," Vexler said.

She pushed the pink button and heard a big and terrible sound echo through the underworld.

A door was opening to the world outside, a *big* door. Iron was sliding and gears were turning as Vexler switched one of the monitors to Tunnel 21. The camera pointed up into the open sky, and for a brief moment, Vexler smiled at the stars and moon overhead. She hadn't seen them in some time.

But then something very large and unexpected fell into the hole.

"Is that . . . ?" she couldn't quite believe what she was seeing until the thing falling into the hole went right past the camera with a look of terror on its face.

A forty-foot chicken was falling into the Dungeons of Snerbville.

"This is a very bad idea," Vexler said.

Vexler had only seconds to activate an inflatable landing area, which was only used when a live creature was tossed into a Snerb hole. If she had been paying closer attention to the monitor, she might have noticed one other important detail that was destined to change the Dungeons of Snerbville forever.

Someone was riding the forty-foot chicken.

ACKNOWLEDGMENTS

Thanking people for a book like this is the pits! And for once, I mean that in a good way.

To all the fine folks at Blackstone Publishing, thank you for supporting a book about an armpit. That took some guts! Speaking of which, let's do a book about guts!

Dan Ehrenhaft, this might be the one and only time I'll spell your last name correctly. I can barely spell to begin with, and that thing is a doozy. Books are so fun with a travel buddy, and what a fun time we've had! You get all the jokes and make some of them better and it turns out you're also a really good book editor. Good job you!

To all my writing buddies for so many years of support and ping pong and candy on a long and perilous writers' journey: Peter Lerangis, Wendy Mass, R. L. Stine, Jon Scieszka, David Shannon, Joe Purdy, Rachel Lipman, and D. J. MacHale.

And for all the help (past, present, and future), these books are always for Karen, Reece, and Sierra. May our journey lead us home!

ABOUT THE AUTHOR

Patrick Carman has authored forty novels with over five million books in print across twenty-three countries, including the 39 Clues series, the Skeleton Creek series, the Land of Elyon series, and the Floors series. He is the creator of After-shock, a #1 fiction podcast on Apple and iHeart, and cofounder of GoKidGo, where he created hit scripted shows *Bobby Wonder*, *Lucy Wow*, *Floozeville*, *Whale of a Tale*, *Snoop and Sniffy*, and *Story Train*. Mr. Carman is an inexhaustible public speaker who presents at events including the National Book Festival, the LA Book Festival, and the American Library Association national conference. He has spoken live to over a million students at over three thousand schools across the country.

THE **ANIMATED** SHOW!

That's right - there's a **BONKERS** show!
Join Jenny, Fen, and Barker as they
solve big mysteries in the town
of Nevermind. It's super fantastic,
amazing, and great! You'll love it!

FIND THE SHOW HERE:
www.bonkershq.com
SEE YA THERE!

CURIOUS ABOUT WHAT'S GOING ON INSIDE COLOSSAL CHEMISTRY?

The **BONKERS** animated show takes place **INSIDE** the most mysterious building in the town of **NEVERMIND**.

With tricky puzzles!
Fen Stenson dancing!
Herb the Snerb!

It's all happening in the

BONKERS ANIMATED SHOW!

www.bonkershq.com

Keep reading for a sneak peek
into Bonkers book two,
Attack of the Forty-Foot Chicken!

Available June 25, 2024

CHAPTER 1

HI THERE,
I'M BARKER MIFFLIN

As you can see by the chapter title, my name is Barker Mifflin. You may have noticed me hanging around in a story called *The Terror in Jenny's Armpit*. Jenny is a pal of mine who had some trouble with her armpit, so I tried to help her out. I mean, let's be honest, most eleven-year-olds just aren't prepared for trouble in their armpit, especially the kind of trouble Jenny was dealing with. It's times like these when you need someone like me around—but we'll get to that later. Right now, there's something a little more pressing I need to tell you.

I'm riding a forty-foot chicken. It's like riding a horse, only it's a chicken, and the chicken is forty feet tall.

I can understand how this might sound hard to believe. But for an eleven-year-old survivalist like me, it's exactly the kind of poultry pickle I've been preparing for my entire life.

I saw this coming a mile away.

But Barker, you say, *you're only eleven years old! Were you really preparing for terrible trouble all the way back when you were two?*

I shouldn't even dignify that question with an answer, but I will because we just met.

Of course I was prepared for disaster when I was two years old.

And I'll tell you why: because when you're two years old, a lot is coming at you (like forks and spoons and carrots.) Danger lurks around every corner for a two-year-old, and the world could go pear-shaped at any moment. There is no better time to be prepared than when you're a human baby. Sure, I'm stating the obvious. A normal onesie-wearing human infant is a defenseless blob of skin and bones. So consider this a warning: do not be a bundle of useless baby! You're better than that.

When I was two years old, I took naps with one eye open, I wore floaties and a bicycle helmet to bed, and I lined my crib with trip wires. And why did I do these things? Because the house could flood at any moment, the light fixture could fall off the ceiling, or a zombie could wander into my room. And I was ready for all three.

Since we're on the subject of me being prepared, here's the first of many famous Barker Mifflin adages you will find scattered throughout this book. I call them Survival Nuggets, not to be confused with Survival Chicken Nuggets, an amusing dinner game my little brother likes to play.

Barker Mifflin's Survival Nugget Number 4, written when I was two years old: *Your first mistake was thinking bad things wouldn't happen.*

No truer words have ever been spoken, am I right?

I'm not sure if I mentioned this already, but the giant chicken I'm currently riding through the woods is chasing a fully grown llama that's about the size of a pigmy goat. So yeah, I'm having a strange and confusing day. But like I said, I'm prepared.

But how did you find yourself riding a forty-foot chicken, you ask, *and where did it come from?*

These are excellent questions.

Survival Nugget Number 117: *The answers are out there; all you have to do is ask.*

And so, since you asked, I will give you the answer. The answer in this particular case is going to require me to go back two days and start from the beginning. But don't you worry, I'll still be out here riding a giant chicken that's chasing a tiny llama when you catch up.

And so it begins.